Unwritten
By Ashraf Shah

For Daffy and Keisha.

Bad move.

1

Tom Hubanach knew the Cheltenham garden plaza; it was almost home to him. He had been drinking here since before he was actually allowed. When he was twenty he had managed to bring down dozens of friends to the Plantagenet suite on the thirty-eighth floor for champagne parties. He was on first name basis with every senior member of staff and most of the cooks.

There wasn't much of a crowd in the lobby. The season had died with the end of the summer and now it was regulars which comprised of cheating husbands, cheating wives and couples trying to cheat on each other with each other in strange new rooms.

The Cheltenham was a friendly place; it was the place to go when there was too much going on at once for one man to deal with.

Herringham was bringing over a set of drinks for Tom alone. His neighbors stared in coy amazement whispering under their breath, quiet and mocking. Tom didn't care, it was his home not theirs; they were tourists here for the service, not the light that lived inside this faded palace.

The lobby bar was loosely aligned with the rest of the space; but it sought to seek out its own place amongst the lavishness. The hotel lobby was a long train of Nouveau architecture, swirling patterns and plush rugs that didn't cross over into the bar area; the line was drawn for them there.

Where the men sat, with their whiskey and tonic water, was the hard, pure, black of tables and dim lights; alluring but private. This was the bastion of those who crawled away from the outside, to the plush cave of the over fed.

Under the red and purple lights of the dim cavern the faces that surrounded Tom Hubanach were not welcoming. All that glowed were eyes under shadowed brows. The white shirts that peeked out from black coats lacked throats because of the darkness.

The Christian bartender glowed under the orange lamp halo as he polished a pint glass with a sparkling white cloth. He valued his work and was absorbed in the crystal gleam; his polishing was disturbed when a red leather jacket blocked Hubanach's view and made an order.

The red leather jacket sat on wide shoulders; it was crowned by short brown hair and a sculpted haircut on a pale skinned neck. The order was made but the back that Tom saw remained. The customer never glanced left or right and decided not to search out the co conspirators that shared this sidled excuse for a tavern.

The Bartender served what looked like a Manhattan and walked back to his polishing. The specter in the red jacket stayed at the bar, standing erect.

Half of the tables were empty; there was even a booth to Tom's right if the specter ever wanted to sit down. But he didn't, he finished his drink standing and signaled the bartender for another.

The Christ-like bartender under the halo of orange came over a second time, leaving behind the stack of glasses that begged his attention.

But the specter decided differently he stepped back and stretched out his arm, he didn't let the cocktail glass touch the bar. He turned in one movement; swiveling from the ankles and headed straight for the booth.

Hubanach looked straight into his face but he could see nothing. The light that had lit the red jacket to a flame avoided the specters skin altogether. He wandered to the booth and sat facing his interrogator. Hubanach's eyes returned to his own drink.

The specter was still bathed in the dark. Hubanach faced forward but through the corner of his eyes he could feel the darkness peering at him. He decided to finish his drink before he returned the glare.

He was at the bottom of the glass counting down the seconds waiting for the moment to catch glimpse of the face behind the flaming red jacket. But it never came.

The specter had disappeared. The glass was there with a box of red Willesden filter and a lighter that sat neatly stacked on the table.

Hubanach looked around for the vision in red but he couldn't see him. After a few moments he wandered to the bar and ordered something else. As he came back the red coat crossed the thresh hold and returned to his seat. Hubanach had missed the features again.

Tom was getting restless now, the face was either avoiding him on purpose or he was getting bored. He was ready to leave when a sound cried out of the darkness.

'A little early don't you think?'

Hubanach looked over and made out a chin and a pair of lips above a red collar. 'Early for what?'

'Cheers anyway.' The specter lifted his glass.

'Yes, cheers.' Tom returned the sentiment and wondered why his first response had been so defensive; the specter was only being friendly.

'I haven't seen you here before?' The specter was adamant in forcing familiarity into the air.

'I've been coming here for years; it's just lately I've been busy. And yourself? do you drink here a lot.'

'As a matter of fact, no. I'd never heard of this place till this morning. I was down on the main road looking over the rivers edge when I heard someone walk past me talking into a telephone saying that they were heading to the Cheltenham. I turned to look and it was a well dressed old man in a bowler hat. I haven't seen anyone wearing a bowler hat in years, so I followed him.' the specter raised his finger and pointed across the room. 'He's over there with a woman to young and happy to be his wife.'

Hubanach wondered if he had bumped into a lunatic. 'Are you some kind of investigator?'

'No, I'm just a private citizen with a spare morning.'

Tom tried not to laugh, 'Tom Hubanach, pleased to meet you.' Tom raised his glass from across the floor; he still had no idea what the man looked like.

'And what is it that you do Mr Tom Hubanach? If you don't mind me asking.'

Tom thought about it for a moment, the last real job he had was Filing clerk in his fathers office almost seven no six years ago. Since then he had spent his entire week wandering from room to room trying to write a travel guide about Bhutan. 'I'm a secretary, but I do a lot of travel writing.'

'Anything I might have read?'

'Only if you travel from Germany and Switzerland' Tom lied most convincingly. 'Most of my audience are European's so I write mostly in German. And you sir what do you do?'

'I'm a collections agent in Burton.'

Tom looked around and wondered if the man in the bowler hat was a bad debtor. 'So what brings you to London Mr?'

'Pat Rowley, But call me Phillip.'

Tom thought about the names Patrick and Phillip, wondering what kind of sick human being would call their child Patrick Phillip? 'Ok Phillip, what brings you to London. Are you on a job?'

'I have an old friend in the city, she hasn't heard from me in a while and I'm here to put things right again.'

'That's nice to hear, I have lots of friends who I haven't spoken to in years but have always thought about them, I still consider them to be friends even though I can barely remember them at all.'

'This is different, the person I'm looking for was once very close to me, we shared a lot of time and even lived together for a while. We were once as close as family. So it's not just a passing acquaintance.'

Tom didn't like the sound of that; there was something possessive about the way he spoke. It was though he were referring to the present with the gloss of past tenses, hiding some unchanged feeling. 'She must be quite a woman for you to still feel this way.'

'I wouldn't know, she hardly ever told me a thing about herself, we lived together purely as two people without a past, I didn't tell her about my life before her, and she didn't tell me about hers. The rules that we wrote for one another were applied purely to the present.'

Tom was getting confused, how can you spend time with someone and have no ideas as to their past?

'All this shouting is......, would you mind if I borrowed half of your table.' The specter was already standing when the sentence came out of his dark face.

'Please do.'

He came over and finally Tom got to see the face that had eluded him for his entire stay at the bar. 'So you were talking about a friend of yours.'

'Well you see we came to the end of our tenancy and she had decided that with the end of our contract came the end of our time together. I didn't really understand what she meant at the time, because I thought that we would still have something after we stopped living together. But I was wrong. On the last day she hired a van and decided to move five hundred miles south, never looking back.'

'That's a sad story, but maybe it was just what she had wanted all along.'

The specter was a pale brown haired man. His nose was small and straight, his eyes were hazel green and they sat evenly with a menacing clarity. His lips were thin and un-chapped from the thousands of cigarettes that had passed over them. 'I want to see her and try and make things right again.'

Tom thought about Cerys and how he had once thought about her leaving him, the thought frightened him half to death. 'That sounds………..' Tom didn't want to offend, 'you obviously cared a lot about this woman otherwise you wouldn't be here talking about it.'

'I've done it again haven't I!' the Specter smiled from over the rim of his glass 'I've turned out my inner thoughts in the middle of friendly conversation.'

Tom smiled. The menacing eyes of the once specter had turned inwards. 'Don't be so embarrassed. I was a bartender at university, I spent most of my weekends listening to grown men tell me about their wives and girlfriends. How long ago was this anyway?'

'Eight years.'

Tom hesitated. 'Has there been……………… anyone…………………… since?'

'Yes I've been married twice but I always seem to return to the same thought.'

Open doors.

2

It was a bright morning in crisp September, the cold bit his skin as he walked through the field on the fringes of town. He had turned up his collar while he walked on the edge of fallow fields. Behind him as distant as a cloud stood a farm house in which he had never been before.

He had walked past countless times but he had never been urged to stop and look in, there was nothing amusing that caught his eye on the rare occasions he walked by, while the sun was preparing to assault the day.

Past the farmhouse for a mile in an eastern direction was the motor-pass embankment with its swallowed roar of traffic and skid marked skin of tarmac.

By the embankment there were the last remains of a man's overcoat tucked inside a plastic sheet. Chris Rowney had some habits that never left him.

Ever since he was a baby he had always hid and concealed things of little value. He kept his money on a dresser but hid his socks under the drawer.

He pushed on through the field wandering down towards the looming cities edge of council estate sprawl but till he crossed that line he still had the comfort of open space all around him. He looked at the faded farm house.

As he walked past, he confronted a sleepy Dog that looked at him, sniffed the air and fell back to its grumbling, he had met the Dog many times, he had once rubbed his fur on a warm summer morning. It was their agreement ever since they first met. They never exchanged a sound or a greeting, only a look of recognition.

Rowney had always tried his very best to stay away from the house, he walked on the tip of the yard wall and walked quietly.

But for some strange reason he had found his way barred by a pile of fallen wall. As much as he tried, he knew he would have to change his route. He walked around to the back of the house and came within reaching distance of a window.

It was dark inside; there was nothing to look at. He knew that there would be someone awake, farmers lived before sunrise, it was only after the light rose that they relaxed, as though fearful that it might not come if they waited.

An electric light came on and a fractured shadow passed the window. It was a man, he could tell by the weight of his dark half. Industry was coming alive right now; no doubt there were cows or chickens that called him out of his farmer's warm hovel and most probably away from his warm wife's bed. Rowney had never seen her but he was sure she was here; he had seen her clothes outside and at certain times, even smelled perfume among the shit and barley.

Rowney could never have been a farmer, but he was sure there was peasant in him and probably a shipwrecked aristocrat too. He was sure without doubt of all these things because they were unchangeable; that was their comfort, they were set in stone. It was only here as he put one foot in front of the other that he was uncertain.

He stood still for a minute and thought about what the farmer would say if he was confronted at his own doorstep before sunrise. Rowney wondered what the man would say to the sight of a strange face. What expression would he find? Would he run inside and bolt the door? Would he be friendly and feed him bread? What could Rowney expect?

The door opened, it was betrayed by the rust in its hinges and the wooden handle click gave it away.

Rowney was in the mist before the door opened and the farmers face remained a mystery till the end.

3
For some reason or other, he had decided to wander down toward the enclave of Ashton road. He had not called or arranged anything, he just decided. It was unlike him to just turn up like this but he felt that he had to.

Across the busy thoroughfare road, stood the Kadiz grocery store. Its yellow letters smiled at him and the vegetables that sat fat under the sun visor overhead, invited him toward them.
On the counter a plump young boy sat with a cap sitting on the peak of his skull. The boy was used to the meat shop smell and turmeric taste of the air; this was a priveledge Rowney couldn't indulge in.
The young face on the till was familiar to Rowney just as Rowney's was familiar to him. Rowney had watched that face grow into its plump shape over the past five years and he was sure that he would watch the plump face shake off the baby fat that hung so lovingly.
Rowney walked through the door and the eyes behind the till watched as he passed behind the shelf full of Basmati rice.
He was heading toward the back. Behind the butchers counter stood hundreds of jars containing Tex's patent Jamaican jerk chicken mix and endless rows of tinned aubergine curry; beyond the condiments stood the upward passage.

The butcher, a heavy old man drenched in dried blood hardly lifted his eyes as the odd shape wandered in through the door marked staff only.

Through the beaten brown door there was a upward stairwell that lead to a flat that was occupied by the one and only Amer Azaz Senior.

The flat on top of the grocery store was all but two rooms. Both of those had been opened so that the whole space was wide and the door gave itself away an entire kingdom inhabited by a television and a sofa.

Amer Azaz was sitting with a cigarette in hand and a rigid smile on his face. His gray hair was unkempt, his gut poked through the space where his vest ended and trousers began.

'Sit down Rowney and keep quiet eh? I'm trying to get this bloody number down.'

Rowney had often wondered how a mind of such infinite wisdom could inhabit the body of a slob.

Rowney drew his eyes to the beaten up television that sat opposite Azaz as it gave away the race results from an Irish derby.

'Bastard horses, lucky I don't gamble with money otherwise I might be down a penny.' Azaz smiled through his cracked black lips and looked at the wandering white man in the crisp blue suit. 'I've told you a million times now, don't come here dressed like you're on a cruise liner. You've seen the boys round here they look for an excuse to smack a head or two. Why would you invite something like that?'

Rowney wondered if Azaz was still playing that old game that he cultivated with everyone stupid enough to look up to him. 'You know what these boys are like, they get jealous over everything, can't pretend now can we? And besides, that skin your in hardly does you any favors around here does it?'

Rowney wondered if this routine had ever worked. 'Have you ever thought that I only wear it when I come to see you? How do you know I don't spend the rest of the day kitted out in Nike's and Burberry?'

'Tartan and air bubbles would never go with that accent. Don't have to be Noel Coward to know that much. So, have you run out of turmeric powder or was there some other reason you wandered in?'

'Just thought I would come and see you, it's been a while.'

'You talked to me last week over the phone; we sat about for a half hour talking about Bruges. What more do you bloody want from me? My spare day with the horses too?'

'Azaz, we have a problem, I can't sit around in hotel rooms any more, I've been at the West Reading for a month, and even though it's the best place for a meeting it isn't so good if you want to bring company.'

'Since when do you think that I give a shit about where you sleep at night? It's bad enough that I give you a third of all the best deals, now you're telling me that I have to find you a house as well? Get out of here, go find an estate agent.'

Rowney stood with his hands folded over his chest. 'I don't want some big monster, just somewhere quiet here in Ashton that I can use if I need somewhere for myself.'

'Well if its quiet you want, why don't you take this place? I hardly use it. The only thing is that you have to make sure that boy of mine isn't smoking cigarettes around the back. I've been finding cigarette butts but I haven't had a chance to slap some sense into him yet.'

'I'm not getting into your family squabbles; I've got too much going on right now. What about the Yearton house that we used last year. You remember the one where we met Stevie last September?'

Azaz knew which house but was reluctant. 'That house is in use, at the moments. It's my drop off point and it has eyes all over it. The last thing I want is for you to be walking in and out at all hours of the day bringing all kinds of new attention on my head.'

Rowney considered this. 'Fine you give me the keys to your Trenton house flat and I'll look after your Dogs while I'm there.'

'Sold those dogs last week, can't seem to find any use for animals anymore. But you can have Trenton. It's just sitting there anyhow. What about our other things how are they? I might as well get a report while you're here.'

'Bruges is going like clockwork and Portsmouth is ticking away nicely. That 42 we had last week has disappeared into the ether and we have good sack of change that needs to be chopped up.'

'Talking of change, I heard you hired out the Terry Melton place last week, heard you had four hundred people in there drinking on the house. It's none of my business, but you know how I frown over that kind of thing. If I got word that quickly, how long do you think it will be before someone else starts paying attention? Look Rowney, a little discretion is what I'm suggesting. You get what I'm saying.' Azaz, fat voiced under shriveled brown skin whispered his advice quietly, and whenever he whispered you always knew it was more then just that. His eyes would draw away from whatever it was he had previously been concentrating on and his words would swallow anything that might be distracting the listener. 'You get what I'm saying don't you Rowney?'

Rowney was out the door and on his way. The butcher stared at his back, he knew the pale face, he had spoken to him many times and it was not unusual for him to bore holes into the expensive suit and the skin it was slung over as the faint sliver of Rowney disappeared into Ashton road.

The butcher put down the cleaver and wandered up the stairs. He reached the top and rattled the door lightly, 'Azaz, Is it alright?'

'Yeah, come in Gafoor.'

'Did you tell him about what I told you about?'

'Yeah I told him, it's all straightened out.'

'What did he have to say for himself?'

'He said it won't happen again, He's a good lad. He knows when he's gone too far. I doubt he'll do something like that again.'

Gafoor looked over the room with its bare walls and the graying carpet that was once so clean and fresh. 'When are you going to let me clean this place up? Ever since I got here it's bothered me. Can't you at least let me get onto someone about this carpet?'

'Never mind that, whats it like downstairs?'

'A few people came in and bought some little things, still got a pile of mince sitting there, its starting to attract flies.'

Azaz looked away from the screen and stared into Gafoor's eyes, he wondered if there actually was anything behind those dull features that stood behind the counter all day. 'When I say whats it like down there, I mean outside. Is that van still across the street? Is there still a group of under-cover's sitting in the chicken and chip shop swallowing bad coffee?'

'Yeah of course their still there, their waiting for the phone to ring or something, who knows?'

To the left of the beaten up sofa the telephone sat neatly wrapped up and disconnected, Azaz hated it for its betrayal, he couldn't even ring the premium sex lines anymore because he didn't want to share his heavy breathing with a jury in a court room.

Gafoor stood erect and wondered if there was anything else he could say before he went back down. He looked over the bare room for the last time and headed for the stairwell.

'Gafoor, do me a favor before you go. Get to a phone and call your cousin Altaf, the one with the cab. Tell him to be over at six; I need to speak to him.

4

Outside of Colchester house, under the clear night and on top of the marble steps he sat alone. Behind him, through the white glass doors; men with too much money hustled under the glare of the brass band that had taken the stage.

The horns mingled with the electric feedback of a fender guitar and the mechanized drone of synthesizer patterns. The stage in the grand ballroom was swaying to the finger picking of a young man looming over the throbbing crowd of men and women. Below the electric shaman, the gentle tapping of razor blades on hand mirrors cut through fine china that disappeared through rolled up currency into the blood streams of the rich that stood below.

Waiters came from far kitchens carrying heavy trays full of champagne and cognac, divesting themselves of their loads left and right.

Outside, locked out of his own accord Rowney set little Indian puffs of smoke into the blackness that loomed above him. It was true that this was his doing. It was true that all that were gathered came to feast on him and his profane Eucharist. But he was tired and he wanted no more of tonight.

It was safe out on the marble steps, those inside would never leave the sight of the electric magician, his fingers held them captive long enough for Rowney to catch breath. He would return indoors but only after he had consolidated another night's losses.

Indoors there were heads bobbing from inside of expensive suits and dresses. Inside there were streams of alcohol, inside there were couples heading upstairs past the decorated lions that guarded the spiral stairwell that was caked in luxurious red and gold; culled from some old Aristocrats vision before bankruptcy made a night porter of him.

Here inside the ancient walls of Colchester house, where kings had once slept, stood the fat and greedy, they cared for nothing; they were here for the free wine and drugs on display.

Rowney slipped through a side door and looked around at the shuffling corpses that smiled invitingly. Women quietly stared at the glassy figure that hung on the edges like a deformed puppeteer, hiding strings under baggy cuffs.

Men glanced and raised glasses, while those who did not know, looked around at the by standers; picking out the culprit Rowney who they knew only by name.

Garret stood on the opposite end. Trusty Garret J Sayby minding the minders that ran the show for Rowney. Garret held his head over the bow tie that he should have never worn, it made him look trite; but he was unaware of the endless jibes that came his way from the smiling horde around him.

Rowney considered going over to talk to his number two, to try and loosen him from his arctic posture but Garret stiffness was part of his charm. Rowney forgave his partners sin from across the floor.

Through the main door new faces entered. First there was a crowd of girls, tucking expensive purses under their arms, sweeping past confidently and devouring the view of every man around; from behind them older men, the patrons of pretty girls everywhere. A top hat on one, a bowler on the second placed over immaculate suits and the faint echo of a butler within shouting distance.

Rowney disappeared just as a group of women were heading toward him.

Through the back doors of Colchester house there were sealed rooms that sat full of viewing screens. The owners had been kind enough to let Rowney have the Keys when he persuaded them to let his teams secure the building for the weekend.

Normally Wallace Hearton wouldn't have allowed an external organizer to have freehold over Colchester but Rowney, as per usual, filled the rich mans ears and pockets with dog eared bills; tattoo's of an ancient queen on her throne.

He stood behind one of the camera operating security guards and studied the mad revelry of the people who claimed his friendship as their own.

Upstairs, twelve of the twenty bedrooms were engaged. One lurid scene in crystal clear black and white showed an old man being ravaged by two blond boys and a black girl. In the other room's needles and hand mirrors littered the floor while the ancient bed frames gave way to the weight of three and sometimes five people, soiling the once crisp white sheets.

A lone bottle of half drunk champagne sat in the hall waiting for its owner to return from the bathroom. A boy walked past falling from side to side in the red hallway, he leaned down and took the bottle to his breast.

The forty screens all told their tales with monochromatic clarity, smiles and frowns littered the wall of pixels in front of Rowney. The seated security guard sat bored, waiting for someone to steal or break something expensive.

Outside a hundred shining cars stood lonesome under the moon, their drivers had disappeared and the security guards that patrolled, shared cigarettes and laughed about the inside of the old house that was being dragged out of its stupor by a hundred angry hornets.

Rowney had climbed up to the view over the roof and held his hands against the ancient turrets, that had stood since men wore powdered wigs.

The floating sound was too powerful to be contained inside the cavernous walls. The sound floated up from underneath.

The noise drowned out the singer and laughter followed, cackles and heckles rose from the rooms below.

Rowney's suit was a crisp blue over a purple shirt; his shoes glittered like the hand mirrors that littered

the big oak paneled bathroom in the back of Colchester house.
 He looked over the green vale that was as black as the world above and let it take him inside itself.

5

When the morning was over and done with, the cleaning crew was still working at full speed. Garret, with sleep filled eyes watched every hand that swept or cleaned.

The workers were all Polish and African; they had come on a minibus at seven o clock in the morning to help every trace of the night before disappear. They were fresh from long nights of sleep and cared not for the things that had happened here.

Every once in a while a stray figure in a crumpled suit wandered out of the big door of Colchester house fumbling for keys and covering his eyes like a vampire in the sunlight.

The cleaning crew kept quiet about the smashed glass and the spilled powder. They emptied the rooms of their broken receptacles and moved methodically through the house, returning it to its ancient exhibited splendor.

Rowney had disappeared at five o clock in the morning. He had left Garret with strict instructions to return the house to its original condition and settle the account before organizing a new venue for the week after. Garret had been the chief of staff for two long years and didn't need to be told twice.

Rowney had a habit of disappearing after a long night. His time among the moths lasted till the last throws of the night. He had no time to watch them leave; battered by the dawn rays.

Garret watched the last cars leave before midday. Wallace Hearton had sent one of his own staff to make an inventory of damage and filial costs above the agreed price. Garret didn't argue he settled the account and left behind that big struggling behemoth of brick and plaster to the surrounding acre of wood and grass.

6

Rowney was in an office for a change. There was no one else there, just him and the old furniture of a cab drivers office.   He was surrounded by makeshift chairs and a beaten up desk with thousand year old phone numbers scratched into the cheap soft wood.

The clock said eleven and the drivers who were freezing outside the office wondered where their boss was.

It was a Tuesday, the twenty third to be precise. The missing fat Polish man who should have been present an hour ago was nowhere to be seen.

Rowney was on a round. He was here for Azaz. He didn't usually perform collections, he left that to Sayby and his lower orders but Azaz had asked for Rowney to personally talk to Marcin Borowski.

Borowski was a wonderful warm human being; he had come to England in the spring of 87. It had taken him ten years to find and accept his place in the world.

When he first came he had dreams of the great exhibition hall he had read so much about. When the old brushes lost there luster and the oil paints lost their shine he did what everyone else did. He found a cab and started to drive. He learned to talk, flirt, smile and earn enough tips to start something under his own name.

The Evergreen cab stand had been opened in 1997 and it had one Taxi. His girlfriend Ayesha operated the radio and Marcin drove. His success came purely from the fact that he canvassed every neighbor he had. His big mouth and friendly ways allowed him to lord over his local pub 'The Parrot,' and its clientele. After the first three months, he hired a second driver and cleaned up in his own neighborhood. The problems started in the summer of 2000, Marcin made the mistake of taking on partners. He made friends easily and turned away none so when one of his drivers offered to buy forty percent of the business in exchange for a share of the profits, Borowski welcomed the investment. It was wonderful on paper but ambition drove the road home. Marcin's partner was called Rehman Bhatt.

Rehman was the hardest working man in the midnight world. he squeezed a penny till it looked like a pound and when he worked hard he demanded results. Ambition drove Marcin's tiny five cab firm into the sights of the biggest local competitor in the citywide area, Diamond Cars.

The monopoly firms of the past had always known of their rival Borowski, but had never seen him as a threat till Rehman flung the doors wide open.

The Rivalry finally led to cab drivers scuffling in the streets and vandalizing each others cars; but the bigger problem came when a group of opposition drivers smashed the Evergreen offices before Christmas of 2001.

Rehman was in the office at the time and had been caught in the middle of it. One of the opposition had thought it clever to bring along a switchblade; it cost him dearly.

In the scuffle Rehman had gotten hold of the knife edge and buried it inside two men. He wasn't looking at was he was doing but buried it nonetheless.

At the trial Borowski was asked to pay damages and Rehman's share of the business had to be liquidated. Borowski tried his best to buy out Rehman but in the end went outward to find a new investor.

Rowney was here waiting for the last two months take. Azaz had no more time for this, it had been a year and Borowski had been making excuses for dropping profits every month.

Borowski had made an effort to run but he was running out of ideas. It wouldn't be long before Azaz really came down on him.

Borowski was parked around the corner in a purple Vauxhall Cavalier. It wouldn't be long till his time was up. Whoever was sitting in his office whether it was Sayby or one of those other gorillas, they wouldn't wait forever. The next stop would definitely be Ayesha and the house. Marcin had to get out of the warm car and brace the cold.

'Please, just let me speak.'

'I'm just here to pick up some money.' Rowney spoke without adjusting an inch from the comfortable spot he occupied, back to the wall and feet on the scratched desk.

''Tell Mr Azaz I don't have it, but I will have it. I just need to sell a few things before I get hold of it.

'You're going to have to tell him yourself.'

'Wait please, I would rather you did it.' Borowski smiled meekly. 'Please, what is your name?' he held out his hand.

'That isn't important I'm just here to pick up, next time it'll probably be someone else, so my name won't help you in the slightest. I suggest you pay up and get it over with.' Rowney's voice never pitched above a soft rumble in his throat.

Borowski looked around at the small cramped space. Behind the nameless man was a small piece of wood that one of the cab drivers had left out of some paranoid self defense impulse. All Borowski had to do was get past the man and then it was a simple matter of splitting the strangers head open. Thoughts of Rehman crept in right away.

'Can't I speak to Mr Azaz myself and work this out some other way? I think I know how but I need to speak to him first.'

Rowney had played this conversation a thousand times. 'Why didn't you call him last week? That wouldn't have been so hard. I know you have been busy, your phone is always engaged and you've got your priorities in a mess. If you owe you should pay. Why should we make exceptions when all you do is show discourtesy by avoiding us?'

I wasn't being rude, I was just busy. Please tell Mr Azaz that.'

Rowney took his expensive shoes off the desk and put his hands straight into Borowski's left bulging pocket. 'This here looks like a fragment of what you owe. I'm going to count this in front of you and I'm going to call Azaz. You're going to explain why you're short.' He weighed the bundle in his hand. 'This is definitely not seven thousand pounds.'

7

Tom was with Moira. He held her little hands buried in his own. He was looking down on the broad sheet of black hair that sat on her head as she looked at the floor cross legged facing him.

Tom was like her, it didn't matter that they had nothing to tie them. While she was busy wondering why the electric frog danced on its back between her feet, he was turning over the origin of her thick black hair.

Never had he brought it up with Cerys, even when he was forced to drag it out into the open by his Mother and Father who laughed in his face every time whiskey entered the equation; he kept quiet.

She wasn't his. It didn't matter how many times a day he looked at her hair and wondered where it came from, there was one simple fact; it didn't come from him or anybody like him.

Cerys was out again. It was her day to work. She didn't need to or even have to; but she still did. Three days a week at the Open-top Gatehouse on Cranberry Row; in the big ugly City that surrounded them.

Tom didn't like it very much, in fact he hated it. Why would she work when they had everything that he could give?

When she married Tom she had asked two things, in the hallowed presence of Mr W Willimer of Welby Wretton and Willimer, two conditions hewed from legal rocks.

One was the obligatory prenuptial agreement. In the event of divorce it asked Tom to divide up all earnings since the date of marriage equally amongst them with a further deduction of forty one percent of any savings to be put in the name of Moira Hubanach. The second was that Tom was never to spend any time locating One Andrew Shah Greston; Cerys's only known living relative.

The great cloud that was her life before Tom, was thankfully where it belonged, contained within a long day in the Hubanach study with a taut old Solicitor for company. Tom was glad of that. He had fought for her and won. Those around him had protested and argued against it, but just for the one time, he had it his way.

Even though there were days when he wished he was still that child who listened to his mother; he knew that he would never willingly give up what he had for anything other then this.

Cerys picture looked down at her two loves on the red floor; they played and laughed as they always did, behind smiles.

It was late when she came home. Tom must have been out with Moira because the house was cold and echoed her expensive heels melodically. She waited for the day when her house on Grady Road would be covered in mashed potato and pencil marks; but it never came.

Between Tom and Angelina the maid, there wasn't much chance of Moira getting loose and tearing holes in the carpet.

Instinctively Cerys flicked her hair loose and pushed her green eyes to the mirror, expecting thin lips and perfect skin to look back at her; but they didn't. She screwed up her eyes, looked through the doorway and wondered what had happened.

The floor was excessively clean, even more so then usual. The chance of an autumn leaf getting past the front door was a rare occurrence but Moira's little feet always dragged a little dirt inside. Angelina wouldn't have noticed as she never did in the afternoons. Cerys had learned this on the rare days she was home. Angelina worked the house over between 9:30 and 12:00, after that it was Moira and a few clothes to press.

This meant two things. The mirror had fallen and was either outside in the Garbage, or had walked into one of the other rooms.

Tom like most men was not immune to a little vanity. When they first met the scuffed corners of his mirrors meant that they left their hanging hooks quite regularly. Tom had most probably been posing in front of the mirror, admiring his ever plumping physique under the light of the upstairs study, forgetting to bring it back to its right place.

Cerys put her coat on the hook to her right and wandered to the steel kitchen at the back of the house. She looked around for the unfamiliar cups that Angelina, no doubt, had moved somewhere new. She pushed the switch on the kettle and looked down into the cutlery drawer.

The knives and forks were gleaming, they sat perfectly in place. The tea spoons shone with odd scratches on their tips where Moira's new teeth had left marks on stainless steel.

There were two televisions in the house, one sat up in the Attic with Tom's things and the other in the living room.

They had a rule; all eccentricities were kept in closets. The only one exempt from this rule was Moira, her toys wandered everywhere. If there wasn't a toy horse in every room the little black haired girl shied away thumb in mouth and eyes to the floor.

Tom kept his Trains upstairs, and Cerys kept her photographs in her study. Her Coney Island snapshot that could have been taken in 1870 and not 1980 sat proud on the wall behind her desk. It was the only image she had that contained a trace of Andrew Shah Greston, The other living human besides Moira who shared her blood.

The photograph was of a bench in front of a Ferris wheel with a fedora alone on the planks.

Cerys hardly ever looked at the picture anymore; there were more then fifty black and white photographs of places such as Java, Kashmir, Cancun, Japan, Vladivostok; places she could hardly remember herself. It was only Tom who was able to smile at each picture, glad to have been there with her when she made them.

But he hated the fedora on the bench. 49 out of 50 was a good score to have but Tom hated the odd that kept him a point below a half century. It was the one image on her wall that he was jealous of, it was the one image which he could not touch.

The phone rang as the kettle boiled over.
Cerys walked to the stand and looked at the ridiculous telephone that she had always disliked. Tom had picked it because it reminded him of the telephone as it once was; a strange wonderful contraption that spoke its own language with every turn of the dials. She picked up the heavy black handset and heard Moira's laughter in the background.

'Hello? Cerys.' It was Tom.

'Hi Tom, where are you?'

'I'm at the A&E, Moira had an accident'

'Accident? What happened?'

'Don't worry, she's alright.'

'Did you let her out on the road Tom? I told you about that before. You're so'

She just cut her finger. The mirror in the hall fell down and she picked up a shard.'

'And where were you when this happened?'

'I turned my back and'

'What about Angelina? Where was she? I knew that you would be letting her get away with not doing her job.'

'Angelina drove us. It wasn't her fault and besides Moira's fine. Look we'll talk some more when we get home.' He let out half of an "I love you" but she had already put the put the phone down and walked back to the kitchen.

8

Sayby was alone again.

He was sitting down in the middle of Great Orton Park. 'It wouldn't be long now' he thought as he glanced down at the ridiculously expensive watch he was wearing. His hands were raw from the bad weather and the dandruff that always took over his head, showed heavily against his black coat.

His only prayer was that the bench he sat against hadn't acted as a urinal for a passing vagrant; the smell of dried piss was terribly hard to get out of a new coat.

He was waiting for a package from a certain Henry Connors whose real name was Amin Tajik. Amin had the fortune to have been born with blue eyes and light skin. He looked like a perfect slightly Slavic gentleman and it got him out of the usual parody of outsiders in general; it also allowed him to wander freely in the strange netherworld of Europe unnoticed. Henry Connors was a pimp and pusher who dressed like a liberal buff, complete with a Guardian newspaper under his arm.

Sayby detested him. Behind his back he always muttered 'sellout' but that was another matter all together.

Sayby was cursed. He had the misfortune of being born a militant; he had all the hatred in the world stored inside him ready for a child's night dream of revolt that never came. 'Garret J Sayby' a name so ridiculous it only belonged in a charity store novel or on a church bulletin board. But Garrets Revolution had ended in 1994 when he fell in love.

He had spent his whole life hating those who he imagined, sought to keep him down. It wasn't his fault of course; it was the perpetuation of a myth that had become an undertone, not just for him but for everyone born within a certain set of circumstances. If you were poor, stupid or just didn't belong, you took a myth and turned it into the undertone that your feet used as the marching beat of your whole life.

Garret fell in love and that was the end of his revolution. He fell in love in front of a rich Ablemarle hotel in London, by the Royal Academy.

He was watching a well dressed man treat a good looking woman to cake and coffee when it happened. Sayby watched the man for the fragment of a second but it played in his head for a year. It wasn't the woman or the man; or in fact the cake or the coffee. It was the expense that swept him from his feet. He had never before lusted after anything. He used to boast about an occasion when he gave his shoes to a vagrant in a doorway that had his feet wrapped in newspaper. But this was different, the glittering moths around the cake and coffee had danced before his eyes and he knew that he wanted that sensation. He wanted to know what it was to have no cares but your own. He wanted to taste selfishness in its full glory.

And here on a park bench, he was doing what he had once despised. He had worn his black band with pride once. He had smashed open the heads of pushers and pimps in an attempt to clean out his own housing association neighborhood; but here he was a grown man on a park bench dressed in selfishness, swallowing like a fish in a filthy tank.

Henry Connors waddled over. His waddle was wasted on Sayby; he should have been a fat man. The waddle would have caught the eye of laughing school boys everywhere; but on the sullied fake Slavic it just looked odd.

'Do you have it?' Sayby never pleased anyone with pleasantries.

'Of course.'

Sayby looked him up and down from his seat on the piss soaked bench that went undetected by his cold flared nostrils. 'Hand it over'

Connors sat down, smiling under those high awful cheekbones that none can stand but cameras adore. 'Sayby, when are you going to invite me over?'

Sayby sucked the corner of his lip and looked at the Slav, hiding none of his anger. 'Listen to me you fucking pimp, the minute I let you in I have to deal with a thousand foul mistakes. Letting you in would be more trouble then even I can manage. Our arrangement is one of stand and deliver. I want nothing other then to make my ends meet. If I wanted a careless idiot for a partner you wouldn't even have to ask. Now be a good boy and hand it over.'

Connors who was still unsure about the name he had chosen for himself, laughed with both eyes on the ground. 'Sayby if I wasn't in love with your money you greedy shit, I would gladly put you in misery; but, lucky for you, I'm kinder then I should be.'

Sayby raged under the blank stare. His coat hid the clenched fist and the raised breath that was ready to make this pretty boy pay. 'You do what your good at and keep with it. I'm not making any promises to you about anything. Right now I have a thousand things to take care of and entertaining pimps to fictional enterprise isn't one of them. So now would you get to the point you stupid fuck? Hand me the envelope.'

The Slav still smiled even though he had been insulted by a man whom he thought was far below him. 'Here are your precious notes you demented bastard. If you want some cunt I can get you any taste you like, even black girls, on the house.' He raised his right hand like a crooked politician. 'But next time I want an explanation, I don't see why I should tail some arrogant icy bitch just for a few hundred pounds like a blind man. Next time I want some identity papers, otherwise, no more deals.'

'Get out of here you pimp, and stop calling me, if I want anything I will get in touch, so don't get your hopes up.'

The Slav, humorous as always got up and shook himself of the dust he had acquired. 'Say hello to that pretty wife of yours.'

Sayby looked at and knew that the Slav had another trick yet to pull. 'Get out of here.'

Henry Connors walked away whistling, as the dew painted his shoes and the empty park echoed.

9

It had been a busy weekend for Altaf. He had been awake for three days, Friday night was a fireball, his cab was always full and he had his fair share of pretty girls that were short of cab fare. The weekend had been good. Altaf had come away with four mobile phones, three watches and eight purses. That was why he only worked weekends.

When he started on the gypsy cab circuit he was clearing four hundred pounds a week. But then his partner, an Irishman called Redding, got caught without a license by the borough. So Altaf decided to leave the gypsy cabs to the Gypsies. Redding got a thousand pound fine but Altaf got away with his livelihood intact.

Four years later, Altaf worked three days a week and cleared eight or sometimes nine hundred pounds on his lonesome. He worked 60 hour shifts and in his year and a half hadn't had anything but a busted tail light, caused by one of his own kids and a cricket ball.

It was Sunday morning and the last of the drunkards had gone home. The sun rose swiftly while the white lines ran through your veins. Altaf had one more stop to make. The clock was just about turning over to seven am when he pulled into Ashton road and wandered over to the Kadiz food store.

Even though it was a Sunday Amer Azaz had demanded a regular hour of opening for every day of the week, he wanted to drive out all suspicion that any might have against him. He was outside in the cold everyday, taking counts and making sure that only the best merchandise came off the delivery truck.

Altaf parked across the street and wandered over to the white coated business man in the morning air.

'Amer Lala, how are you?'

Azaz turned around and waited a moment before he acknowledged Altaf. 'Altaf just let me get this and we'll have this straightened out, ok.' Azaz carried on for the rest of the hour while Altaf read the Daily Jang newspaper, fresh off the delivery truck.

Azaz flipped the kettle on and took of the coat he had been wearing. Altaf was already seated when the voice gave out its instructions.

'Altaf, do you know Rowney?'

'The white guy.'

'The young one with the brown hair.'

'Yeah I know him, whats he done?'

'Nothing, yet, but I want you to make sure that it stays that way. I've been hearing some unsavory rumors about my little friend. It turns out that he has a thing for debauchery.'

Altaf didn't know what debauchery was but he guessed it wasn't good if Azaz wanted a tail on his golden goose. 'What exactly has he been doing Azaz?'

'Well a couple of weeks ago he hired out the Melton rooms in Gatesmoor and had a guest list of two hundred people, all drinking for free and snorting too.'

Altaf thought about it, those kinds of parties were dots, you had the odd dark face dotted here and there but mostly for decoration. Yes, even in this liberal world a splash of color on the edges made more sense then a room full of it.

'When you say tail, do you want me to ask about or follow him around? I'm a working man Lala, I can't just drop everything on your say so.'

Azaz, always humorous and comic, got blunt all of a sudden. 'I hate reeling off lists; I believe it's rude to constantly remind people of their debts and vices. So don't make me rattle my brain for yours. Everything we have worked on has always worked out in your favor, I don't have to remind you of that. So do this for me and I'll make sure you're looked after.'

'This Rowney, what is it you think he's doing that has got you dressing in white? I'm not prying but you know that this spying thing never works, the last time you set me to this, we found out a whole lot more then we needed to and lost a good man because you were up in arms about his personal habits.'

'Anybody with something to hide is never a good man to trust with money and it wasn't his personal habits I was offended by. It was the lie that mattered to me most.' Azaz was adamant in this.

'Alright what exactly do you want me to do?'

10

It was a sad sight to see but it was there alright, plain as day or dreams drawn on paper.

'If you just give me another few weeks, that's all I'm asking for.'

'But that won't achieve anything; there's nothing that you could possibly give me that would make me change my mind. What do you have that you think would make me forget what you owe?'

I have a house that's got ten thousand pounds left on it, if I sold it I could give you the forty thousand as a down payment on what I owe.'

'But that's not enough, I've plowed three hundred thousands pounds of my own money into your cab stand Marcin, Do you know how long it took me to gather up that much money? Do you even care what it cost me? Doesn't that bother you in the slightest?'

'Mr Azaz, I don't have that kind of money, I cant just say I can get it because I cant, not all together at least, but what I can do is pay as much as I can in small doses, its fair and its regular and its what I can do.'

'So what do you think I was letting you do before? I wasn't being unreasonable, I wasn't asking you for a lot, I was only taking what you owe, but because I was kind, you took that as weakness, and now you're paying for that assumption. And don't pretend as though you don't know what it is that you have that I want. It's not as if you're completely without assets. You have fifty one percent of Evergreen Cabs. And right now it's your last card; I can't really see anything else that you have that's worth pursuing.'

'That's not fair, you can't ask me for that, its all I have to show for my whole life. That place isn't just walls and a switchboard, its everything I've worked for and its everything that I have ever pursued. I don't see it in terms of profit and loss; I don't look at it that way.'

'Well then maybe it's about time you did, because I have been reasonable with you. I have sat down countless times to try and make you understand that liberty costs more then bad debts. It's a matter of ideals, and once you start to question another mans ideals, you question his very core. And I can't have people questioning that. So if you owe you should pay, just like everyone else.'

'Well I cant and I'm sorry.'

'I'm disappointed, you have made me come out all this way on the busiest night of the year. You have made me crawl on my hands because I am fair and you have only made me realize that fairness doesn't pay. So it's entirely down to you that I make this decision. Everything I am doing is a reaction to what you have done.'

'What are you going to do?'

'My representatives will be in touch. Till then I suggest you think about what you're doing. Think about the benefits of my offer and the damage that you will do yourself if you don't take it. Goodbye Marcin, I'd like to say it was good, but that would be a lie.'

11

Rowney had the whole plane to himself; he was heading over the Channel accompanied by a pilot. He was wanted for a meeting in Calais; the tourist port was open to the beer runs of every Englishman. Between the endless rows of beaten up vans and trucks that lodged the bodies of able men; was the little siren of Rowney's fortune.

At the port of Calais a woman was waiting with an envelope, inside the cheap brown envelope was a letter for Amer Azaz. It was coded of course so even if Rowney uncharacteristically opened it, he wouldn't find anything but the engine specifications for a brand new Mercedes.

Rowney met the plain woman in a little café on the coastal walk and spent less then three minutes drinking the watered down piss that passed for coffee. She smiled at him and then sucked down the hot vapor quick enough to leave him with the bill.

Every time he saw her it had been the same, she would hand him the note and then leave him with the bill. Virginie was crafty like that, she had no time for a man without manners. She wandered out of the café knowing full well that Rowney didn't have a Euro to his name and as always, she didn't give a shit. Her boss paid her for courier services not courtesy.

The return journey could wait. Rowney was in the mood for some casual avoidance. He was fluent in French and his time here had given him enough confidence to not be mistaken for a tourist. He watched his fellow Englishman as the marketer's robbed them for the little coins they had and went freely without being bothered by the street vendors.

He wandered over to the cobbled streets of old Calais and watched as the tourists flashed their digital cameras at bored looking Frenchmen.

Café culture was over rated; it worked for the French because they had no reason to escape themselves. It was only islanders that needed that vice. The isolation of the sea forces men to lose themselves if only for a few hours. Neither side could agree and any politician that sought to graft the social habits of one country upon the other was only fooling himself and no-one else.

Rowney had told the pilot to go back, it was not out of fear that he shook off the quiet pilot but a longing for the ocean, he hadn't sat on a boat in at least a year and his occupation didn't allow him to wade in the water. So today he chose to wade out of defiance.

The black channel bounced the Ferry like a newborn. Rowney stayed in the belly of the ship in the center of an overblown shopping mall. He balanced a cup of coffee against his knee and watched a good looking woman drag an ugly child from store to store.

All around him good looking smiling women dragged their unhappy brats back and forth, back and forth; rocking with the waves that carried them.

Rowney counted down the three hours he had to share with the daylight world till the anchor landed at Dover.

12

'Look at me Rowney. I'm not talking to the thin fucking air here.'

'I'm sorry but I can't help you, what I do in my spare time is my business. How I spend the money I make is nothing to do with you. There is nothing that I won't do for you Azaz but if you think that you can control me when I'm not on the clock then you're mistaken.'

'Last week a policeman came into my store, do you know what he said to me? He told me all about a party in the Tirean rooms where a fourteen year old girl was sexually assaulted by three men in a back room. He gave me all the filthy details and he even showed me a report of the girls blood test result. She was filled to the rim with amphetamines and alcohol. Imagine that?'

'What has this got to do with me Azaz? You dragged me out of bed to hear horror stories? Stop wasting my time.'

'Well you see Rowney, last week the Tirean rooms were closed for refurbishment's, I know because I own a fifth of them, I own that place so if anything untoward happens there it gets back to me straight away. Now last week at about two o clock in the morning the rooms were filled with three hundred people all dancing away while there was still sawdust on the floor and nail guns everywhere.'

Rowney knew that the game was up, it was foolish of him to have assumed that he could use the Tirean rooms for a floating party it was one of the most reckless things he had done all week.

'Now what I would like to know is why someone would attempt to do something like that knowing full well that the Tirean rooms were off limits? I would really like to know what kind of a reckless person would attempt something like that?'

'The Tirean rooms are off limits I understand, but that doesn't mean that they were closed to everyone? I had to get hold of the place, it has the best security system of any closed venue that I have ever seen. Its one of my personal interests, I have always been drawn towards recording devices.'

'I've known you for six years, you were recommended to me by a friend of mine in Liverpool, he said to me that you were the best man for long jobs, and he was right. In the time you have been in my service I have depended on you for some of the most sensitive of missions. I have made you privy to some of my most private dealings, I have managed to re-circulate into actual business and legal enterprise more then I ever thought possible. But this is something of a hazard. I've known about your sideline for about a year now. I've known about what you get up to at the end of the month and I have known about all the prostitutes you spend your time with. I know this because it's my job to know about my employees. If I'm going to trust a man with everything I want him to be able to trust me as well. But you seem to lack that openness which keeps us from becoming indomitable. I respect a mans right to privacy as much as anyone else but if your planning to use my premises then I would like to at least have some foreknowledge. And one more thing I want recordings.'

 Rowney wasn't in the mood. What he did in his spare time was his own affair, he shared everything with the fat old man but he didn't really want to share this. This was his own personal enterprise, this was his release, this was where he went to disappear. 'I cant help you Azaz, what I did last week was very stupid and I admit it and in future ill do my best to keep them away from you. I'll do my best to keep out of the city and away from anything that ties them to you.'

 'You don't seem to be listening to me, you can do whatever you want as long as you inform me first and because I have a few ideas of my own that I think would work well under the cover you are providing, I want a piece. What you don't know Rowney is that every time someone makes a recording in the Tirean rooms security office, downstairs in the basement the mass recorder makes a duplicate, the only person who has access to the mass recorder is me. I can go down there at any time and find out whats been going on. And this is precisely what I did after I heard that you used my club for a private enterprise.'

 This was not what he wanted to hear, a lot had happened in the Tirean Rooms last week a lot that Rowney didn't really want to share. He liked the dark because it kept its own secrets safe but if that same darkness encroached on the daylight it revealed an uglier side. 'What do you want for those tapes you have, name your price.'

'Price? No I don't think you understand, I don't want to extort you, I want to be a part of it. I saw some familiar faces on those tapes. I saw a few faces that I have seen before; only whenever I see them their dressed in blue blazers, posing for cameras. Your grainy footage showed them snorting cocaine off a child's limp body in the ladies toilets. That's what I'm looking for. In this world that Is worth more then gold. After all we are living in the most watched country in the world. I feel like I want to watch to.'

'Those people on that tape trust me; they trust me enough to turn up every time they are invited.'

'Listen to yourself, they come because you pay for everything, they come because no one else will have them. They come because they think you're a soft touch and if you want to be seen that way then that's fine. All that I want is your cooperation in laying a few traps. I have a friend or two on the gossip sheets and they're always looking for political trash, they're always searching for good rumors and do you know what the great thing about a rumor is? It never runs out of breath. It just keeps on running.'

13

Edgware Road, that haven of ochre cast-off's from the east of a once Arab world bustled nervously. Here and there, the headscarves and moustaches bobbed up and down freely and as fast as black cabs. The green neon lights of restaurants named after pretty girls glimmered in the winter air.

All around, the dark of the city was coming down; enclosing the resident and the lost tourist as one undistinguished thing.

From amongst the foreign castoffs were a pair of shining shoes and a long coat over a once Irishman, also a cast off from the little finger of Europe. He was also one of them, the far flung son of the first and most unruly outpost of the Empire that had rebuilt itself.

There among the pomegranates, he roamed in painfully new shoes. He had worn them after much deliberation; they had sat underneath his rack of coats for eleven months waiting for him to return to them. Before they were his, they belonged on the shelf of an Italian Shoemaker. At the time he had wanted them like a new love, but he had failed to consummate till today. So like any new thing unbroken, they tore into his ankles and took away the thin skin over his heels.

He was searching for two plasters that in his stupidity he had forgotten. He saw them every day and had forgotten, through familiarity, that they would have to be broken before they would befriend him.

He looked everywhere for a pair of plasters but he didn't find them, not at least for another mile in the hustle of the cities vibrant winter street.

But sadly he didn't have time, not this time anyway.

He didn't expect this to happen, not here, not now.

He had made plans, he had constructed a precise routine he had rehearsed and thought about how he would approach her, he had thought himself a slither, he had thought himself sleek and friendly, but if he didn't think fast he would walk straight into Cerys who was loaded with bags and walking straight at him in his hobbled state.

Cerys had been out all day. She was out looking for clothes and a new book to read. On the Edgeware road was a little store that kept pretty pictures of the Oman desert. She had often wondered what it would look like with her own eyes, and once she even bought tickets to go and see the grace of golden sand for herself. But that day had gone; some other thing had taken its place. Some other distraction had gotten in her way. She remembered what it was, it was that man she had once known, that sad faced Irishman that had held her down while he told her so.

He had told her that he was hers and she had been taken in by that. She had believed him when he said that he belonged. But she had never said that she had belonged to anyone; let alone him.

She knew his name but she did not want to say it. She had repeated his name to herself a million times but it didn't bring that first feeling back. Every time she thought about him something was stripped from her memory, almost as though he were a photograph thumbed to many times. So in the little bookstore she dared not say it, she didn't want to smudge the dim blurred image anymore.

Rowney ducked left behind a newsstand, dreaming that she had seen him and would turn around to his darting shadow. But she didn't, she kept on going.

She was wondering about Kathleen her neighbor who had recently lost her husband to a younger man. Cerys had always suspected Theodor; he was hardly hardly discreet about his duality. All Kathleen had to do was leave the house and an alarm would go off in the mind of every unsavory character within a two mile radius, telling them to congregate by the ground floor palisade, in broadest daylight.
Kathleen was upset but not enough to act irrationally. It was a sad loss to find her husband of twelve years telling her that he was leaving her with a mortgage and a clump of debt; while he spent his time chasing pretty boys all over France and the Spanish peninsula with his 'companion' Terence, as he liked to call the grinning dyed blonde idiot that he had chosen over a devoted, loving wife.
Cerys carried on, her moral maze of sad generalizations always hit her hard. She didn't mean to judge but sometimes it just came to her. She shook off the gossip of her home street and carried on walking.

The shadows under head scarves locked eyes with her in almost recognizable smiles. The faces opposite her on the street, especially the women, thought about nodding or smiling at her. After all in the dim light she could have almost been a tall Yemeni lady, her cheekbones and full lips certainly hinted at it to her wandering admirers.

From the right of her eyes under a bright yellow marquee for an eastern blockbuster a black coat flashed past her, she stopped mid step and wondered where to place her shoes. For the flash of an instant she almost stopped right there to look at the abrupt thing that had passed her. There was definitely something, she felt it pass. She knew it to be there. But carried on anyway, walking as though she had just seen some familiar but unfamiliar thing in the falling darkness.

Rowney put his hand on the wall and looked at the back of the tall slender woman who walked away and wondered if she could feel him behind her; if there was some way that she knew. If some scent or recognition had set off something in her mind. He quickly dropped the thought as absurd and stood looking in both directions losing footing, forgetting the pain in his feet and letting them step toward her. He quickened his steps.

Cerys was heading toward the tube station that sat on the far edge of Edgware road. she hated the tube especially at this time of night, it was littered with sweaty businessmen and the odd lost teenager dolled with an expensive blazer and shined up shoes, no doubt with a modern classic by Hamilton or Bukowski under his arm.

She knew that she would have to sit while a sweaty man sized her up. She knew that the smell of the cab would be of leather and plastic, she knew that the winter would stifle the air down in the network tunnels.

She fought the need to jump in a cab; she was in no mood to sit in traffic. The station loomed around the corner and she let her feet do the work. Her gloves kept her fingers and the big gold band hidden. She thought about taking off her gloves but that would not deter the gazing and the running eyes that would run over her.

She walked to the gate and got through the first time. The city was kind in that way, it knew and recognized her as one of its own; she didn't need to fight with the inspectors like tourists and school children. She was a friend, a welcome friend at home in her own world.

Rowney was all out of change, he hadn't ridden a tube in months and he didn't need to. He lived on the black cab and the personal driver. But here he was, fumbling for change which he knew he didn't have, wondering if his roll of fifties had ever been as useless as it was right now.

She was ten paces ahead of him and he was definitely sure that he had caught the eyes of someone as he followed her. To his right and old lady shuffled through her purse for the ticket that she knew was there. Behind him a noisy group of schoolboys who parroted a TV wide boy accent within note perfection, spoke loudly about things they had not yet seen or done.

The shadow he chased kept on at a pace.

He wondered quickly about how to get through. He looked at the old woman and stopped her. 'I'll give you fifty pounds if you let me have that ticket.'

She looked at him and gasped. 'Sorry young man, I have to get home I have guests and if I miss the next tube I'll be late for my own appointment.'

He looked her up and down and couldn't believe her. Fifty pounds was fifty pounds it didn't matter who she had round for dinner, any fool would take the money without a second thought.

He turned around and stuck his hand out to the Mockney wide boy in school tie and trainers. 'Here's fifty pound for your ticket.' The puppy fat face didn't need to be told twice; he took his friends to the nearest arcade and returned home three hours late, welcomed by a leather belt and an angry pair of parents.

Cerys sat on the train with the good fortune to be first on, it was 6:14 pm and the tube was a sardine can. Opposite her sat a thick eye-browed young man with high cheekbones and a days shave on his face, he had brown eyes that sat clasped under heavy lids, 'the weekend had taken its toll' she thought to herself. He was clasped in a brown leather jacket and Dr Marten boots that looked heavy and ponderous. He was busy staring at a blond girl with a fringe. He looked over lovingly as though he knew her but she didn't return his regard, she was busy with her own friends who laughed at her every joke.

She could feel the dreaded eyes on her already, it was a bespectacled man that had started on her fingers but had now worked his eyes to her throat. His suit was off the rack and in a way it was her own fault. She had stared in his direction for a full thirty seconds at the blackness outside the windows, 'poor man must think I'm staring at him' it ran through her head but she quickly dismissed it and him.

She had a million different things on her mind, like the horrible smell that was coming from the lady on her right. She smelled cleaning products. Bleach and hand soap oozed from her neighbor, it wasn't unpleasant, just, overpowering. She was so used to the sweat that lingered in the air, that being in the vicinity of a virtual chemical plant overpowered her. She tried not to show the effect on her face, she looked around at the standing and the sitting and then she felt a second pair of eyes on her.

Rowney had managed to catch the tube a moment before the doors rolled shut. For the first stop he rode with his coat tail outside the carriage. He kept his back to the door and hoped his embarrassment was private.

The carriage was a box of workers, all on their way home, he could have caught a million different stories out of them if he wanted but decided to look for her in the shuttling tin can he temporarily called home.

He passed his eye over every head of black hair; he looked over the faces and tried to find her.

She wasn't on the carriage. She must have passed him and gone to the next one.

He turned his neck to the next carriage and craned in with his sharp eyes searching out the face he sought.

The next stop was hers.

The electronic voice called out her home and she grabbed hold of the bags at her feet. The eyes, that she still hadn't detected, were glued to the side of her face. She knew they were piercing her skin through the glass of the next carriage but the ruffled coats and crowded doorway prevented her from getting a clear look at the dark eyes that looked out.

She stood up and those that surrounded her shuffled back apace. The eyes of the tired and the standing prepared themselves for the warm seat she had vacated. She didn't look back but she knew that her seat had already been taken by the brown haired girl that had shifted her weight seven times from foot to foot and side to side.

Cerys took hold of her things and marched up the platform, the crowd that had cleared for her as she stepped from the carriage huddled in the doorway and jostled for space, she calmly walked away, imagining nothing of the all too familiar scene that unfolded behind her.

It took Rowney a few moments to realize that she had gotten off; he knew that it was one of the two stops but he had imagined it to be the next one. He saw the glimmer of her hair and the gray bags at her side. He slipped through the closing doors like a serpent.

He had to control his feet as they raced close to danger. He forced the hands downwards that sought to grab her shoulder. He was close, to close he thought as he forced his heavy breathing to lightness; he didn't want his game foiled before it had begun.

He followed her at a distance and kept to the corners making sure he looked away whenever she looked back.

Cerys looked at her telephone, she had four messages and one missed call. Tom no doubt, telling her about some strange new thing that fascinated him, or maybe that Moira had done something new; Tom was like that, every hiccup and smile was an event to him, She was grateful for that. It had been one of her great fears that Moira would grow up without love. Cerys didn't want that to happen again, once was enough she didn't want that for her own daughter.

Rowney kept back and watched as the statue rose on the escalator. He watched the living graven image climb higher and higher, over the arc till she disappeared.

He sped his feet and ran up after her. He reached the top of the moving stair and looked around. She was heading out of the north exit and he wanted to give chase.

He pushed his ticket into the barrier but it flashed red. He tried again but it was the same. He watched from inside the barrier as she disappeared. The coat trailed behind her up the stairs and that was that, she had gone again.

'Do you mind getting out of the way, your blocking the gate.'

Rowney went back into the dark.

14

Burned out shells of buildings were beautiful things when photographed after a war. They made majestic advertisements about the horror of conflict and the debt the present owed to the past in eradicating the possibility of it ever happening again.

It was only in peace time that burned out shells were laid out for the drab things they were. It was only in peace time that you could wander into one and have nothing but contempt for those that dwelled inside them. It was only during the peace that you could spit on an unwelcome habitant and still not care about the feelings of others.

The council had once sent in the Force to shove out the homeless from the drug maze of burned out complexes on the Freedleton marsh Estate. A miniature riot had burned black hole eyes in the face of the four storey complex and the once foolish few that dared stay were long gone. Left behind, were the last remnants; the last of the dead, the walking or mostly sleeping dead.

Reza was curled under an old mattress and a pile of newspapers. It had been two weeks since he had slept on a real bed and now while the sun was coming down he felt the familiar rumble in his gut. He needed something and if he didn't have the convenience of a petrol pump less then a mile away he might have starved. Next to him sat a half open tin of spaghetti and a few slices of bread. He polished off the tin and found his way through the window and door-less flat that had been burned a year ago, by a mob in retaliation for the arrest of one of their number.

The dead riot, which was eulogized by a few discolored fire burns on partition walls, was part of an attempt by the local police to detain a twenty year old man on an assault charge. The assailant was halfway to the adjacent squad car when his mother intervened and received the blunt end of a night stick. The sheer spark of the blunt object started an electrical storm that burned out fifteen apartments and four police cars. It was a sad thing that had happened, Reza slept among half burnt toys and Mickey Mouse wallpaper. Everything was re-usable, a different dream to the infants was tenant here. Heroin painted the nightmares of a lone man and his thoughts were housed in the last of the last.

Any smart thief knew that street robbery was madness in the city. It was the most obvious form of stupidity left in the world. It belonged to the hooligan and his girlfriend. It belonged to the cowardly few who had more balls then brains. It belonged to a dying breed.

A smart thief who wanted to reach the end of the week without seeing the inside of a cell kept to the edges. The metropolitans had worked wonders turning boom town into tourist heaven even with the prospect of mad Pakistani boys dreaming of trees in the sky.

It was just the way it went; a quick hand was no fun in the daylight. On an island so small, the potential for trip hazards doubled. The chance of having your entire fuck up detailed and narrated on some third rate CCTV digital spotlight TV show on cable, was no prospect at all. It was once a novelty to be on the news but now it was the last thing you needed.

Rez wandered out of the city to the nice quiet towns that wanted to be London, who knew why. He wandered to Watford, Staines, Dartford anywhere that wasn't loaded with eyeball cameras and overgrown bullys in black and whites. He wandered through the boy racer havens of Essex gutting the prize Ford's and Toyota's. He blessed every brain dead nineteen year old in the South East for latching his savings in a cruise machine with an overblown stereo system and bad taste paint job. He gutted freshly painted cars in back alleys took everything he could, leaving shells on bricks.

Reza could have been a great mechanic if he could put them back together. He would have made a beautiful hand in a shop if he wasn't so keen to rob the register. He would have been great at something if he wasn't so keen to disappear.

He loved the smell, he loved it more then the memory of his first girlfriends virgin body. He loved the cheap perfume smell more then the smell of fresh money. He loved the way it was so sweet it made you choke in its opulence. The smell of fire branded heroin was enough to drive him onwards. It was enough to have him rob and steal till there was nothing left worth taking.

In the dark of a back alley on the outer rim of the Wedgewood estate, he tore out Mongoose brand bucket seats from some eighteen year old girls Corsa Sport. He dreamed of the scent of heroin and he thought about the sixteen locations where he could get hold of some.

In the end after he had three hundred pounds in his hands for a scatter of electronic and interior equipment that was at least worth fifteen hundred. He settled for the last number on his telephone, he called fifty one Merchant Street. He called on his old friend Paul Rodry, moonlit Pimp and basketball coach drug pusher to the local youth club.

Inside the beautiful house, all done up in ivory white by the soon to be Mrs Rodry; sat an unfamiliar man in a Boateng suit, waiting. 'Alright mate, I'm Rowney. And you are?'

15

There was no reality in the Drayton room. Especially not tonight, for tonight it was the scene of one of the floating storms; courtesy of Garret J Sayby.

The Drayton room was located on the top shelf of a long white blocked building beyond Nottinghill gate. On the seventh level of the white whale was the Drayton room. An open space the size of a school gymnasium decked out like a ballroom, dimmed like a parking space and filled to the brim with stragglers and detainees.

Rowney was hiding in the shadows as usual, the lowered lights kept the world away from him even though it buzzed with imitative fury. Sayby had filled the hall with forty five of the most expensive call girls in the city. The audience was made up of retired councilors and low level politicians.

But Rowney didn't want to amuse himself this evening; he had been playing cat and mouse game over and over in his mind. The tunnels of the capital had kept him amused for the rest of the night. He didn't leave the underground until midnight and rode around till he could stand it no longer.

He had replayed the hunt over and over.

Even now, as he stood in front of the wall of screens in the smoky security room watching the cities upper echelons run around after half naked girls in the dark, he could only think about the mouse and cat-like pursuits of 20 minutes in the middle of last week.

Terry, the small, unmemorable, seated security man snorted as he watched the silent black and white. He chimed with the steady beat he could hear through the adjoining wall. The entire wing had been reserved, so couples ran frequently from the hall to the bedrooms and back. Security guards walked inconspicuously, given strict orders not to interfere with any of the guests. Again Sayby had made sure that the in house team had been replaced with his own guards.

He was stalking with his right eye, Garrets eyes playing chase all over the place. His ears were being filled every five minutes, the radio piece in his ear hissed and crackled as the silent alarms collected and relayed information back to him.

The end of the world was coming down for someone. They hadn't decided yet. Sayby and Rowney had picked three men from the forty coke addled Governors of the realm to put the hand on. Rowney needed this; he needed the help of those who didn't really want to help.

A month earlier Sayby had managed to corner a rich little girl in Mayfair, the rich little sparrow as it turned out, was sired by a hawk. Those who stalked the realm; heads held high, could hardly control their own households, and now they were going to pay for their laxity.

Garret had learned from the pretty blonde of her fathers ongoing affairs with Cocaine and champagne.

She lay on the king makers bed with a naked Garret beside her, weeping after her tear stained existence. Swaddled in golden robes, in the most over priced room in the capital; she wept about her poverty. The razor blade rattled on the mirror and the black skinned man listened while he brushed away the tears from her makeup spoiled eyes.

'He doesn't love me, can't anyone see that? All he wants is someone to look good for his friends and peers. It's like I don't exist outside of election time. I put on my cream blouse, tie up my hair, smile wide for the camera and hold his hand. He doesn't need us he doesn't even want us around.'

Garret listened quietly as he stared at the thirty foot ceiling looming overhead. 'Don't say that, he's your father, all fathers love their children they just find it hard to admit sometimes. My own father was ....'

'What the fuck would you know?' She leaned over and stared him down fiercely. 'What would you know? He walks around as though we don't exist. He pushes money our way and slips out the back door to any other world he wants. You don't know what its like to love someone so much that you follow them around just to know where they are all the time. You don't know what its like to find out that the one you love is weaker then you, but even then you still can't hate them; Its torment to not be able to decide because you love.' She made a line of white disappear 'and love makes you stupid.'

She rolled back over and let his hands settle on her throat. He rubbed the sharp triangle of pale flesh that sat above her breasts, he fought the impulse to climb on top and make love to her again.

'I followed him once, twice, a hundred times. I looked for him in the same place every time and he was always there. The honorable Andrew Wismith peer of the house with his trousers down and his nose covered in white powder, while two boys fight for his penis with their tongues. Do you know what its like to see your father stretched out like that? While your mother is at home swigging the cooking brandy that she so neatly waters down? Do you know what it's like to know that when your fourteen years old and your father is the only man you have ever loved?'

Sayby had the hardest task, any false word would push her back into a coy shell of sulkiness, so he kept quiet and let her carry on.

'Every week for a year he would wander off and every time I followed and watched him through the penny glass in the wall of the Uranian club on Fletclay row. My father couldn't help but perform in front of an anonymous audience; he had to lie in front of the coin operated glass while young men and women pushed him around and used him like some kind of device. Do you know what that is like to see the one you have loved your whole life do that to themselves? To be subjected to abuse for pleasure? It leaves you a different person. My father, great and all powerful, put through the mill and savoring every minute of it and still I loved him for his abuses; I loved him for his weaknesses even though I had only ever known him for his strengths.'

She was crying as she drew out a line on the mirror, she wept salty tears into the mixture and trimmed a perfect line ready to perform the disappearing act. Her angel face and childish breasts dangled over her knees as Sayby curled up against her back and watched while her hips pushed into his ribcage.

'But I still love him and, and I couldn't refuse him. I couldn't refuse every time he took my hand and we walked through a museum, I couldn't refuse him when we took coffee on the Mile or at Galsworthy house. He was and still is the most important thing in my life.' She was smiling through bloodshot eyes and tear stained cheeks, Sayby pulled her down to him and licked the last tear away, they made love in the morning and then he left her to clear up the room of her expensive and torn dress.

Wismith was in the fourteenth room, he was so full of pills that his feet had decided to go a different direction to his body as the two boys who were behind called him back for more. The swirling electronic sparrow followed him out of the room capturing him with its gray eyes. Behind the sparrow Rowney watched eyeless, he had seen this hundreds of times, he had accounted for many of the most powerful at the worst of times. He had watched on a variety of screens as the powerful let themselves loose at his little gatherings. He had seen the most respected and most high, fall apart at the seat of debauchery. It was all routine.

Sayby was standing in the exact same spot he had occupied for an hour, he had received the news through the ear-piece and now he was glad, he could return to the quiet room that adjoined the others through an exiting panel that was sound proofed. he could wander into the back and read a book while the rich who had no reason to suspect anything more then privacy unleashed could carry on till the sun rose and vampires returned to their coffins.

16

'Rowney!' Azaz was smiling fully.

'Azaz.'

Rowney, you sure have me on a favor. Tell me what you want? Right now I'm in such a mood I could sign over Louisiana. Name your price Rowney and you can have it.'

'Wismith wanted money so I gave him some from the numbers at Heaton.'

Azaz lost all the color from his face. 'Money? You gave him money? From the Heaton numbers? Are you out of your mind you stupid Mick? That isn't a charity box you can just dip into. That's where we pay the Calais star from every week. If there's nothing to collect then our other halves on the French end are going to go somewhere else probably to that Slav that your man, that black runs with.'

'I put it back a week ago from my own stock.'

Azaz frowned he didn't like the unwarranted intrusion. Never did a man, no matter how friendly, give away ninety thousand pounds to cover his boss's loss. 'Why so generous? Why didn't you just give him the ninety yourself and leave the Heaton numbers alone? If you're so affluent that you can pay off those you're supposed to be extorting then why did you need to mess with my routine? You wouldn't have even had to mention it.'

'I thought I should, after all it's your money and all of the business with Wismith is wrapped up in your life, I doubt if it was just me I would have to deal with extortion. I am happy with things the way they are, I don't have to go above and beyond anything that I can't control, I've spent five years as errand boy, and that time I have learned that sometimes the worst kind of gamble is always the most opportunistic. When there is a simple way to win there are always more then one that are out to win. You said that remember?'

Azaz looked at him and tried not to eat his own words. 'Don't worry about Wismith, he has been wandering in the back alleys for a long time, it was only a matter of situation that was going to bring him down. Anybody stupid enough to flaunt themselves as much as he does deserves whatever shark bites they get. If it wasn't me then it would have probably been splashed all over a newspaper.'

'But isn't that what you offered him as an alternative, a career dragged through the mud and a life in tatters, instead of a blind eye over customs charges?'

'I've known about Wismith for a long time, I have been wondering after him for ten years. Do you want to know how I met and found him?'

About fifteen years ago I worked a house in Gradlebury Avenue; it was just a regular den. Gambling, whores, a little pot in the back kitchen. Nothing too extravagant, but I sat around there acting as muscle for a little old white man who had run the house for thirty years. He hired me after I beat the crap out of his previous guard in a nightclub on the Kings avenue Garden. The little old white man saw me tear his prized bouncer apart with only a beer bottle and my size twelve's. I was there making a mess in the dark while hard house music dimmed the screaming and shouting, when this little old man taps me on the shoulder and gives me a card. I'm there knuckles raw and face a red mess; trying to read 4 point lettering on a business card in a dark, strobe lit hallway, while a team of security guards were just about ready to pounce on me.

About a week later I make the call, and the old man pretends like it never happened. He just puts the phone down on me, so I forget about it.

Another week passes and he calls me up again and invites me to a horrible little pub in Wedgewood green. I wander in and I'm surrounded by Doctor Martin boots and shaved heads. I'm standing at the bar waiting for someone to start the shit. So I'm there with one hand inside my jacket and the other cradling a beer waiting for one of these peel headed fucks to grow balls. When a tiny hand settles on the bar. It was the old man he came through, he brought me to a National Front pub to see if I had the balls to walk in and order a beer.

The Nazi's had no idea who I was and if it wasn't for the old man they would have torn me a brand new one. But the word was out; there was a real hold in there. The old man had the power over those overgrown SS clone bastards.

So I'm at this house a month and all kinds of traffic is passing through, everything from two penny heroin addicts on a big score to rich boys down from the hills. I sat down, played cards and talked to most of the girls. The nicest women I have ever known have been whores. There's nothing that you can show them that they haven't already seen. There's no fear in their eyes because the ones that had gotten as far as the Birbeck house knew that this was the end of the line, this wasn't some first time learners club where pretty thirteen year olds got knocked up by old men telling them that they loved them. This was a factory, a fuck factory where you came in the front and left through the back, every penny and every pound was tallied up and no one bothered anyone else.

That's where I got confused.

The old man never got bothered; he played his games, made his coins and kept on going. On a good night he was clearing close to two thousand pounds after pay out, and I never saw him paying out. There was no big boss behind it all; there was no tax man who came with an iron bar or a crossbow or some bastard device to make your life miserable, not in my two years anyway.

So one day I asked him how. "How do you manage to sit in the middle of the most overwrought city in the universe, a city so riddled by territorial lines and taxation; and manage to live independently?" He just looked at me and laughed.

'What do you think I am? Just an old pimp, who sells pussy on the high-wire? This isn't all I do. This is just what I do while I'm retired. I used to be Jack, Jack Marks the High-wheel roller. I used to be right hand man to the Colonel. I was the king of this whole town for fifteen years. I didn't just walk in and set up a knocking shop in the middle of the city free of charge. I bought my way in with my whole life. I own this city because it owns me right back and besides, follow me upstairs.'

So I followed him up to the balcony room. Up there was the main quarters of "Olivia" the crown jewel. She had tits like you have never seen and the face of an angel. Olivia's room was fitted with a big mirror that ran from the floor to the ceiling. It also acted as a two way window where she set up a Ferguson video star camera to film her antics. Old Olivia had a sideline in fuck films so she wired the room for sound and filmed herself with all manner of men.

One of her big draws was junior ministers and civil servants. And that's where I learned about Wismith. At that time he was bounding after the rights of the family and the uniformity of the church, he was riding the Daily Mail right into the big house. Pity though, because he liked to play wife to a woman sporting a giant green rubber phallus.

Olivia gladly pounded away for a change and pretty much devoured those tapes of hers. When I walked in front of that two way mirror I had no idea what I was looking at, all I saw was a woman with short hair being fucked by a skinny man with long hair. It was only when they turned around that I saw what it was. I didn't know who Wismith was and I didn't want to know. Most of the time I kept out of the way of the perverts and bored husbands. They kept to their end and I kept to mine. I only appeared when the panic buttons went off.

'See that young man in there, one day he's going to be a peer of the realm and that's when I will make him mine. If you have been in this game for as long as I have, you will know that there isn't much that can't be done, and there is nothing left that hasn't been done. If you really believe that then you will live a long trouble free life preying on those who believe differently. The reason I'm here and all those men who I once served aren't is because I believe in learning. I believe in the value of history and if there's something to be learned in the world then it's that fucking is the best way to bring someone down. It's when we are at our weakest and it's when we are at our most vulnerable that we best learn to serve a purpose.'

'Now listen to me Rowney, I know that your not used to pulling strings because I've never asked you to have a hand in it before; but I need you to do this properly. Wismith is a big fish, with the habits of a bottom feeder. He has been an arch pervert for as long as I've known him. He's like some throwback Marquee lost in the wrong century, he doesn't care about anything except that parallels remain parallels. If there's something I know about him its that he hates eclipses he doesn't want his two lives to cross each other, as long as he can keep Sir Andrew Wismith Peer of the realm and Wismith the prowling fiend apart then he doesn't care, he is willing to pay for the protection of that name of his; so if we can offer him the freedom to live inside his own cage then who are we to argue. We can give him all the debauchery he can stomach and we can keep the eyes from off of him till we don't need him anymore.'

'And what do you get out of all this? I mean you're not the kind of man to give something for nothing, what is it that Wismith has that you want so badly? What is it?'

Azaz was a little hesitant; he wasn't quite as trusting as he made out. He wanted to give away his secret but only after he knew it was going to come true. He didn't want to give away the game too soon. 'All in good time Rowney. You just sit him down and tell him what we can offer. Tell him that he can have free run over our dens whenever he wants just explain it to him like that and he will do whatever we want.'

17

It was dusty in the warehouse, Garret didn't like it here. There were rows and rows and rows of pallets stacked with dust, they were sitting seventeen rows deep all matching colors and shape. Garret was only here to get something out of the locker stall in the back.

Rowney had told him to go to the back row lockers and get a pair of gloves from locker fifteen A. it was not strange for Garret, he had been high errand boy for two years and these requests for a strange item of clothing stashed away in a locker or under a floorboard in an old barn was a part of the grind.

The warehouse was a second; and that meant that it was a hired workshop in the name of a dummy company that was indirectly owned by Amer Azaz through a series of shares made on his behalf by various law firms and private citizens.

Although it was common knowledge that Azaz could barely balance a check-book, the fat old mans recognition of this minor deficit in his personality had made him very reliant on the mental faculties of his lower orders.

Sayby wandered over to the back and fumbled through the locker stall. He searched out number 28583 and opened up the beaten locker that no doubt held the stench of twenty years of work-men's boots and dull tobacco long ago smoked.

There was no new revelation; it was a fedora, a plain beaten up cream fedora, small and almost childish. Sayby held it up to the lights and tried to imagine the head it belonged to. He gave up quickly. His imagination was a thing sparked by reality; the arrogant daydreams of a Rowney or an Azaz were beyond and perhaps below him.

He wandered off clutching the beaten fedora and passed his eyes over the fresh coat of polish on his shoes, shunning the dust that had clung to them.

Outside, the little purple hatchback sat in anticipation for Sayby to put fire to her, moving her away from the cement and broken windows of the Arlington Sirras Warehouse.

Put aside.

18
'So, Mr Rowley'
'Phillip, call me Phillip.'
'Ok, Phillip it is. Tom familiarized himself with the fake F & L roll of tongue. 'Why did you wait so long? I mean eight years is hardly a short time to dwell on something, if you don't mind me saying it sounds.....'
Tom didn't realize it but those eyes really got to him, those piercing glances the stranger threw across the room to other patrons as though he were sizing them up, as though he was wondering what they would taste like.

'Obsessive?' Phillip smiled through the beam of orange light that seared their table. 'Its just one of those things, one of those all consuming things that makes sense only when you think about it. Like purpose, purpose drives you forward. She is my purpose.'

Tom was getting drawn in, he didn't want to of course. It was absurd. Eight years? What a time. The stranger didn't look a day over thirty, his eyes betrayed more but his face was unmarked. He was young and that was a flaw in it self. 'What was her name?'

Phillip, the stranger froze and the only movement that came from him was the pursing of his lips as he pushed a bubble of smoke over the table, smudging the image that Tom had of him, behind a cloud of cigarette smoke. 'Sarah Louise'

Tom didn't imagine that, he had thought some long and extravagant throttling of vowels; nothing as plain as "Sarah Louise." It was the name that belonged to a niece. 'Did you ever try and reconcile with her Phillip?'

'I lost her the day she left, it was as though she fell of the face of the earth and reinvented herself as something else altogether.'

The scribbler in Tom was filing away, he had no tongue for this kind of thing but somewhere a long time ago he had reveled in the heart break of others.

'So' Phillip said. 'Whats she called?'

'Moira.'

'Not, your daughter.'

Tom sat still. Had he really forgotten? Was his own life that dull that he hadn't realized that he had mentioned and then forgotten about it? How else would the stranger know that Moira was his daughter's name? 'How did you know that was my daughter's name?'

'You mentioned it when I sat down.'

'When?'

'After you talked about your book.'

Tom thought for a moment and then let it pass. 'My daughter, Moira; turns six next year. She's a terror but I don't think I could do without her.'

The stranger ran his eyes over the face he inspected, the sincerity was definitely genuine. 'Family is always good, even when its not.'

Tom had heard that before somewhere, but he didn't really have the kind of mind that can relay a quote to its source. 'Yes, I mean I don't think I'd ever go back to what it was. Sometimes I say I would love to go back to a selfish life, just a typewriter and an alarm clock to worry about but I really wouldn't know what to do without them both.'

Phillip, the stranger was not listening, he was doing a great impression of a listener, an attentive and kind listener but underneath he seethed. 'What's your wife's name?'

Tom wondered, why was it so important that this stranger, this unimpressive vagabond from a lonely table across the room was so centralized in his aims? But he had named her that haunted him so it was only fair that he shared Cerys. He felt a quote coming. 'After all, whats in a name?'

The stranger squinted and leaned forward as though he were about to receive something lower then a whisper.

'Her names Cerys.'

Phillip didn't react at all; he perched for a second over the red velvet and looked at the soft face opposite him. He returned to his original position and banished his hands back under the table. 'That's a nice name, is she Welsh?'

'No her mother was from Liverpool, and her father was a grocer from Cyprus.'

Phillip's eyes ran along the edge of the table right to left.

'How did you meet?'

'That's a long story; take more then a morning to spill out.'

'My days clear. I don't have a thing to do till late in the afternoon.'

Tom was hesitant. He hated to appear maudlin, especially in front of strangers. But there was just some strange need that overtook him, a need to reveal something. If not to glory himself: then at least to gloat over the lonely stranger. 'About nine years ago I worked as a clerk in an office block' he edited out that it was his families own office block, one of thirty five to be exact. 'I didn't like it much, I'd just gotten out of university and I was already exhausted. So a friend of mine took pity on me and managed to find me a room in Liverpool where I could just lie down and do nothing. My dear old......' he almost said dear old father. 'My dear old, boss..... Yes my boss was kind enough to hold my post while I was away. And that's where I met Cerys.'

'You were in Liverpool nine years ago?'

'Yes I was, I stayed there in the winter and came back in January.'

Phillip opened his mouth to say something and then stopped. 'Please, I interrupted you, you were saying.'

'I was in a pub when a big gorilla of a man decided that he was going to barge past me and spill beer all over the place. I moved back as fast as I could but he was already on top of me. I got soaked and was pretty angry so I shouted after him. He obviously wasn't impressed so he came back over and asked me to repeat just for him and the eight friends that he had with him. I backed off.'

'Naturally.'

Tom scanned for sarcasm, but there was none to be found. 'I had only been in Liverpool a few days and I found the accent hard to grasp. So much that was said to me went right over my head. But this man, this thing, from what I could tell; was quite upset that I had called him back. He squared up and was just about ready to kill any inkling of bravery I might have felt, when a head of black hair got up from the nearest table and stepped right in the middle of us.'

The stranger smiled as though he had been a witness himself. 'So you met the woman you were going to marry, just before a skull thumping.' Phillip laughed under his breath. 'Sounds familiar.' Phillip quickly changed tone. 'Bars I mean, strangest things happen in bars.'

Tom got stuck again; he looked over at that strange face that responded so well to the oddest of references. 'Anyway, she steps in and pretty much pushed this behemoth into submission, I wont repeat what she said but I was pretty shocked.'

Again the stranger smiled in some strange acknowledging glance.

'She chased him away and then turned to me, asking if I was alright? I told her I was alright and before I could say anything else she was heading for the door. It was strange, I was soaked in beer, my trousers were just a wet stain and it was broad daylight. On any other day I would have gone into the gents and tried my best to get presentable. But I just ran after her.'

The stranger was absorbed, he had sat with every word as though he were making a measurement for some other fitting or setting.

'She was halfway down the road before she realized that the thumping noise on the pavement my shoes made was coming towards her. But as soon as I got within reaching distance she spun round and smacked me clean in the face, knocking me out cold. It was only afterwards that I got an apology. I woke up in a strange room with a frozen bag of peas over my eye.'

'Ha ha ha ha' the stranger chuckled for the first time. Tom joined in, after all it was amusing; first she saved and then scarred him.

'Sometimes you can see the mark that she left on my face under a strong light. She still runs her hand over the spot almost like you would over an object that you own.' Tom regretted saying that out loud, he had thought it so many times but he had never considered it as an opinion worth airing.

Phillip looked up and stared right into his eyes, Tom felt the poison coming in the next conversation. He was a kept husband and he had known it all along, the façade, the grandness, they were all signs of the kept, he hadn't earned any of this it was all passed on to him through his guardians; first mother and father and now his loving wife.

'There is nothing wrong with a strong woman, Sometimes the best kind of woman is one who knows what she wants. God knows there are so many of us that don't.'

'Cerys and I became friends, we spent a day together while I was in Liverpool, and mostly that was to make up for the beating she handed out to me. It was only when I went back to the south that I started to hear from her.'

Phillips breathing softened, he was no longer breathing loudly he was quieter and absorbed; he was ready to gorge himself on conversation.

'It started with a letter and from there it just grew, till eventually she moved to London and we just took it from there.'

Tom's one man audience sat statue like with a hint of a grin on the corner of his mouth.

'And that is all I have to say, ever since that day I have never regretted a minute with her. And even though we do have our moments I wouldn't ever give her up for anything.'

The afternoon had turned its corner. If the angelic Bartender had bothered to count, he would have noticed fifteen trips that he had made back and forth from the table of Mr Tom Hubanach. The stranger that the bartender didn't know was still there after the lunch hour had receded. From behind the Bar the conversation was a series of open laughs and quiet rumbles. The table was too far away for the topic to leak out to the waiting staff. So the tender tended and the drunks drank on.

19

Rowney had hands like a Hindu god; he had fingers hidden behind fingers. London was hell on earth but the fire was a comfort. In the city of Dis he found himself at home. In a city of ancient stupidity he found himself like a lost son.

He bought into all kinds of things that once upon a time would have burned the skin. When he was a young man he had spent a weekend amongst recovering alcoholics as part of a trainee-ship in medical counseling. One of the things he realized was that it wasn't the substance or the effect that fuelled the addiction; it was the human need for routine distraction.

It didn't matter what the distraction was, as long as it was part of a routine that the body could handle. As long as it was part of an ongoing process it didn't matter how bad it was. All that mattered was the routine. And that was the power of it.

Another thing he had pledged was that he would never get involved with abusive substances; the weekend had given him the knowledge to see that the reliance on routine should be one of interest not apathy; that was where it was best to lay yourself down.

But in the city, under the smog covered sun he was sitting in the hell of a deal maker's room selling uncut heroin to devils in tracksuits.

He sat with men who had lost their self respect to the routine. They were as addicted as their slave customers. For them the routine had become insatiable, it had become a thing in itself.

They all had similar dreams; they all had a magic number that they aimed, for hoping to quit when they reached it; like a thermometer on a hospital charity chart that gets crayoned every week before the total gets filled. But they never did, they either got arrested or they spent the money in one insane act of self destruction.

They would go out and buy a forty thousand pound car or treat their girlfriends to a five thousand pound holiday in the Caribbean; an act of random stupidity, not from ignorance but sheer self destruction. An act of faith is a surefire method of testing the bounds of reality; much in the same vein as the junkie tests Mr Newton by leaping from a window ledge.

Here, within the hell of pounding urban music and the smell of fresh carpets, incense burned and friendly smiles passed around the room. Rowney betrayed his past and made deals with the end.

The chance of escaping was long gone and he knew it. The old myth that said this was the way to the door; was gone. There was no reason to leave. He had finally found something he was good at. It just took him eight years to admit it.

The first time Rowney locked eyes with Reza he knew straight away; all the chances were gone. Reza was the reason why victory and success were so prized. He was the opposite, and every time the winners saw him in the street they understood why it was so important to win.

Behind the filthiest white t shirt and the most beaten up jeans in the universe stood nine stones of pure adrenaline. Reza had spent four hours tearing a one ton car to shreds with only a hammer, a screw driver and an adjustable spanner. He had done this, by his own count, four hundred and twenty times over six years. It would have been a bigger number to boast but those six years contained three six month sentences in rehabilitation centers in Bedford.

In the bright lit rooms of some forgettable drug dealer's house, Rowney found a little distraction. He had been bored for months only he hadn't realized it. He had been unable to see the boredom because he was so busy and in his complete hyperactive state, he had forgotten that once upon a time he had worked as a guide to the lost.

It had been one of the few things that he had ever done, before he got swallowed up and spat out, that had ever left him feeling strangely human.

Here it was again, that old craving, that old lust that wasn't for flesh or coins, but just for satisfaction; some strange unconfirmed need to quench something. Here in Nine stones of bone and sinew was the opportunity to satisfy that old craving one last time.

'What's your name then pal?'

Reza ignored him "fucking wannabe prick" he thought "I ain't begging you nothing so leave me alone" Reza didn't need to say anything, it was all apparent in the glare he pushed toward the man in the Boateng suit.

'I'm Rowney, Chris Rowney, and this is one of my houses.'

Reza ignored him. 'Rodry, you holding?'

Rodry, the host, didn't say anything.

'Like I was saying this is mine, all of it.' Rowney added.

Reza flexed his throat like an emaciated rubber horse. 'I don't give a shit; I ain't looking for no place to live landlord. I'm just here for some personal. So just quit with the chit chat.'

'Rodry's all out, that's why I came round, I came to set him up for the month but old Rodry seems to have mislaid his cash stash or just decided to call it a day.'

Rodry, the third man, kept awfully quiet through the whole exchange.

'What the fuck's he talking about? Man, you got nothing or not? I telephoned you an hour ago and you said you did. I don't owe you no money and I ain't asking for no handout, all I want is a bag for my day off so pass it over and I'll be gone.'

'I already told you.' Boateng suit smiled gently.

'I ain't talking to you Boateng; any one stupid enough to spend grand on a suit ain't anyone I want to be talking to neither. Rodry? You saying I walked an hour to this shit for nothing on a Friday night when you knew there's no one else out there who can set me up on this whole shit estate. What the fuck is wrong with you? Why'd you bullshit me?'

'Rodry's out of business, I've decided to cancel his contract. He ain't working no more; he's going to teach basketball full time. Ain't that right Rodry?'

Rodry, the strange concoction of Black, White and Chinese nodded in agreement.

'You're a fucked up Brer, Making man stretch out in the cold when you know you ain't got nothing. What am I supposed to do now? Where am I supposed to go for my hit?'

'Well I'm off Rodry' Rowney shook off the stray flecks of cigarette ash that sat on his lap. 'It was a good year for us both; I hope that it works out for you.'

'What about you Boateng? Where you think you going? I'm sure that you might have something worth holding.'

'Don't even try it; ask your mate Rodry who I am.'

'Who the fuck is this, Rodry?'

The silent flat faced man born out of some strange love in the midlands twenty five years earlier didn't say more then he had to 'Leave it alone Rez.'

Rowney stepped toward the door and left quietly.

'Cant believe you Rodry, can't fucking believe you.'

Rowney was behind the wheel of a black Mercedes when nine stone of sinew jumped in front of him.

'Wait up' Reza walked to the passenger side. 'Look man, I need a ride, since you is his supplier you might know someone who can help me out.'

'Why should I help you, a two bit junkie that probably sell a kidney for a bag.'

'As long as it was a fat bag, yeah.'

Rowney hated him already, he was one of those crude little bastards that seemed to have evolved

from the remains of the dinosaurs of ten years earlier.
'Get in.'

20

Tom was in the living room. It was a beautiful cold day outside. The big windows let the light in and the lonely sofa that sat close to it was bathed in the crisp winter light. Tom had a cup of silken coffee in his hands and he sat robed from the bath.

Moira and Angelina had gone out for the day; the house belonged to him and Cerys.

They had made love with the lights on for the first time in years. He had insisted that she look at him while he lay underneath her and for once she was smiling; as though this were funny to her, as though this whole comedy had finally found its punch line.

Cerys had forced Angelina out into the cold this morning. She didn't really want to go; it was only the suggestion of dinosaurs that gave the plan a head and a tail. Moira had been watching a man in a purple dinosaur suit sing and dance for all of twenty minutes when Cerys had asked her if she would like to see real dinosaurs.

Angelina put on the big coat and shoes that Moira could hardly move in and disappeared inside the belly of a London bus from the corner of Grady Street.

Tom was looking at the big screen television with the sound turned off. He wasn't paying attention. He was still damp from the shower and hadn't bothered to get dressed. He wasn't planning to change habit all day if he could help it.

Cerys was up on the second floor, dressed in nothing at all. She was looking for a big white robe that she had bought, a month ago. It was here somewhere, she knew, but she wasn't really looking as methodically as she normally would.

'Bring my slippers and pipe dear.' He shouted up to her.

'Maybe in the next life Tom, right now I'm more concerned with heels.'

When she finally came down, she wandered straight into the kitchen and made coffee. The white robe was irritatingly warm, so she loosened the tie and walked through to the living room.

'Tired?'

'No.'

'Good, we have a long day ahead of us.' She sat opposite him on the single sofa. 'It's been a while since we have had a day to ourselves.'

'It has, hasn't it.'

'I can't remember the last time? Was it before I went to Seville?'

'No it was before that, the last time we had a day to ourselves was when we left Moira at Mothers and went up to Leeds to see the Salgado show.'

'There was a Salgado show in Leeds? I don't remember that at all.'

She lifted up the corner of her robe slowly.

'Yes there was, I think it was called "Exodus." He put his cup down. 'It was all about East Timor and Africa, Cote d'Ivoire I think.' He got down on his hands and knees and crawled over to her.

She loosened the other edge of the robe till he could see the skin from her ankles to her throat inside the thick white material.

'Oh I remember, the children climbing from the Sam pan.' Only the thin white tie covered her belly. The rest of her was open to the full view of the giant window.

He ran his hand from the inside of her ankles upward. 'Silver prints most of them. Quite beautiful.'

'I remember them. I remember them all.' She closed her eyes.

21

Waterloo station was a strangled voice, all as one in a sea of white noise. Hundreds of lives accelerating in different directions bubbled over inside their mobile telephone conversations and selfish thoughts of pay day and Sunday mornings.

Every man woman and child circuiting the building was a fragment perfectly attuned to the time they occupied. Every soul swarmed majestically under the brass eyes that looked down. All except for one small dancer running anti clockwise at rush hour.

The little man at the center of the huddle in the five o clock dash for the nearest route home; was the object of spite to every stranger in the building.

In his dragging tweed jacket and baseball cap, he was the tourist's tourist. He dragged a little bag that sat gigantic on his shoulders. The cap hid his face under its oversized beak of a visor. He heard the curses of the suited majority and caught the passing glare of the fishlike commuters swimming upstream. He laughed politely under his hat.

The station was still the same. It might have been given a prettier face but it was still that old cigar smelling dump of old.

The little man dragged his feet to the nearest exit.

He had been on some kind of metal machine for the last fifteen hours; he couldn't even remember where he had come from. With every passing station the old thoughts disappeared, it was as though his memory were dictated by the premises he occupied. It was more then nostalgia it was actual recognition and absorption of one life layered over another.

His guts had tasted the very worst of train cab sandwiches, designed in France but left to simmer in a vault off the Black sea somewhere. He looked for a friendly place to find some real food but all he saw were hideous plastic monstrosities selling burgers and fries. 'So' he thought 'that American causeway has finally dragged itself over to the land of the Angles' he giggled and shimmied out into the moving mass of the street for a breath of London's finest smog and diesel fumes.

It was late in the night when he finally found a place to rest his body; he had walked past fourteen hotels and found them all inadequate. The strap of the little big bag he carried had left a blister on his shoulder but he didn't care, it was the new shoes that bothered him. His ankles had swollen under the black polished exterior he had swooned over less then twenty six hours ago.

The room and the ceiling he was staring at was a fragment of a little bed and breakfast that smelled of cats and tea. He couldn't stand cats and he only drank coffee, but what drew him in was the lack of neon and plastic glowing signs of bargain deals plastered over a huge banner.

He was in his trousers lying flat on his back, in the middle of the tiny bed that was huge for him. Around him were photograph's of a girl photographer with the camera covering her face and a beaten up old box that sat closed by his left ear.

He had been on the bed for the best part of twenty minutes when the door rattled.

'Hello?' he dare not move from the comfortable position he had settled into. 'Who is it?'

'It's your contact.' The voice outside sounded clearly through the cheap door and decided to give nothing else away.

It was inevitable, the little man would have to get up and see the door was opened.

The man had been in the room for all of twenty minutes. He didn't give his name, only an envelope full of scratched unreadable handwriting.

The little man looked over the notes and nodded politely, hardly saying a damned thing all the way through. What came from the stranger was a long harsh monologue.

'We would like from you a way in. We want you to get us inside, we would like for you to help us.'

'I can.' The little man was cut off.

'We have brought you here for your services, not your charms. Once you have completed your task you will be free again to do as you please.'

'And whats the task?'

'Its all in the notes, as long as you read and make clear decisions based on the paperwork you have before you, we will see that you are benefited generously. We have no qualms about how you go about your business as long as the ultimate aims are achieved, do you understand?'

Even though the conversation was as confusing and irrational as the little old man had ever heard he decided to humor his generous benefactors with a nod and a thank you.

'And one more thing' the faceless faced one said before he left. 'You can't stay here, I have a list of four locations which we will prefer you to stay at. This location is inadequate. So please comply and go to the location we have requested.'

Then he was gone, he barely looked at the little man who was on the verge of asking a name or a handle, anything to take away the mad rambling of the last twenty minutes.

The door slammed and the little man collapsed back on the bed.

22

Cerys was frantic. Every store she had been in had proved false; it wasn't long before her feet were nursing blisters and her ankles bled. She sat down in front of a huge poster of a perfectly sculpted boy in designer underwear; she bit into a piece of chocolate cake. She had beaten her record by one day; she had managed to go a month and three days without anything fattening. She had replaced every strange and indelicate snacking function with a piece of fruit or a glass of water.

The rough diet she was on was taking its toll. This morning she had found herself fighting with the toaster out loud because it had swallowed her muffin and refused to give it back and the trainee girl from Derby had caught flack from Cerys after she brought her the wrong coffee. It had been a long and drudgery filled week.

Hub Gentry, the thick and oily clothes magnate from Seville had decided to take his account elsewhere, he had found the Cranberry row offices too provincial for his liking; but the rumor was that he had been enticed by a bigger check from the Yale-Kingsley in Gordon square.

So here she was in front of an over coifed boy in tight underwear staring down at her from his airbrushed height, cleaned up of all the adolescent pimples and chest hair that advertiser's detested. Hairless and bold he looked down at the aging designer as she wolfed down her sugar coated chocolate cake in the middle of the lunch hour; surrounded by school children and working mothers floating on James Last's finest piano accompaniments.

Some genius had set a coffee bar down in the middle of a cross of paths in the Band street Mall. It had little glass sheets to separate it from the malls shoppers and the hard seating was unfriendly to those who chose it over the benches under the fake plastic trees.

Across the open court of the mall, on the other side of the misshapen coffee bar, a pair of fast feet were heading toward the woman who collected crumbs in the lap of her expensive coat.

'Hello Cerys.' His feet were quicker then the time she had to acknowledge them.

In the split second that she had before looking up, she raised a hand to wipe away the chocolate that sat on her cheek; she failed miserably. 'Hello.' She didn't look up.

'So how have you been?'

She was still busy scratching the crumbs of her jacket and hadn't looked up. The voice that spoke hadn't yet given itself away, so in her mind it was still a stranger she was half talking to. 'Not bad, busy. and yourself?'

'Same as always, trying to be good and not succeeding.'

That got her attention. 'She knew that phrasing and she knew that cod Irish accent that softened the end of a sentence for emphasis 'Chris?' she looked up and was halfway to standing. 'Chris? What are you doing here? I thought? What did you? But, but what are you doing here?' the old apprehension came back, surely he wasn't? No he couldn't, he wouldn't be so stupid! Would he?

'I've been in London for a couple of weeks, just wandering, keeping myself busy. I thought I saw you a on a train but I wasn't sure, so I kept my distance. I was just wandering this morning, looking for a new pair of shoes when I saw you and I just knew.'

She didn't want to hear that, he was doing it again; he was foregoing the small talk no matter how much she pushed for him to engage in it. 'So what have you been doing? It's been so long since we last spoke. I hardly know where to begin.' So unexpected he was; so unexpected this was.

'I've got a few minutes spare, would you, I mean if you're not busy; would you like to get some coffee? Since you already have cake.'

'Well, I do have a few things to take care of' What a bad idea she knew it to be. 'But I'm sure I, yes why not.'

Rowney put his hand out and then took it away before she saw what he meant by it.

Despite passing four conveniently located coffee bars, Rowney insisted that they walk out of the complex and disappear down a side road where there would be less noise. Cerys was protesting violently in her head but on the outside it came out as a few mumbled 'I don't mind if, really I don't.' But Rowney dragged onward.

There was little to say when they sat down. So Rowney decided to open up the puzzle box.

'I hate to say it out loud but eight years is a long time.'

'It's only as long as you let it become.'

He looked at her hands, older and chocolate stained. 'That's a nice ring you're wearing. How long?'

'Seven years next summer. And how about you, are you? Are you married, settled down?'

'I came close once but it just didn't feel right.'

That's bad to hear, who was she?'

'She was a photographer in Leeds. I met her through a friend. I guess I was put off by all the expectation.'

How long ago was this?' Cerys was interested; she wanted to know. It was almost as though her thoughts of him were unfreezing right in front of her as she added new ideas to the fading snatches that she had from before.

'It was a long time ago, just one of those things I guess. But enough of that. How have you been? I haven't heard from you in so long. I mean it's almost as though you just evaporated.'

She laughed at that. 'Evaporated? That's an awfully big word.'

'Well I am growing up Cerys; I know it's hard to believe.'

'You look great Chris, happy almost; as though you finally found whatever it was you were looking for. So what have you been doing?'

'I've been doing a little secretarial and collections work for a debtor's agency in Bradshaw. Its funny I mean I remember being chased around by bailiffs but now I'm their own right hand man. Most of my friends are square jawed debt collectors and former doormen. It's quite strange, once upon a time I couldn't stand those guys but now I'm all turned around. Are you still into your fashion design?'

Yeah, Yeah I'm still going on full steam. I've got my own department now out on Cranberry row, do you know it? I suppose you don't know where that is; being a tourist and everything.' She looked at the cigarette packet he had taken out and placed on the table noticing the brand was still the same. 'What are you doing in the city anyway? You haven't just finished kicking in someone's door, have you?'

'No, I'm just looking round for somewhere to stay. One of our major accounts operates out of Islington and they're looking for a new department head and I was thinking about taking the job. I've been wandering around the city trying to get acquainted with it.' A thin girl arrived with two silver cups and placed them before Chris and Cerys,' he thanked the waitress and carried on. 'I've been living all over the place and I guess I'll look forward to stay in one home for a change.'

'Where have you been?'

'All over; France, Scotland Cumbria, Brighton, Leeds obviously and for a short while I was in Dublin.'

Cerys noticed that his hands weren't empty, they were still holding onto something. His nails were cleaner then they once were and his knuckles were still beautiful shards of jutting bone under perfect skin.

He had always been vain about his hands. 'I see that you still smoke Willesden's?'

'Of course, Willsden's as always. Although for some reason they're much harder to get in London.'

She looked around for a no smoking sign. 'I haven't smoked a cigarette in two years; I haven't smoked a Willsden in close to eight years. So would you be so kind.'

He didn't need to be told twice. He had already lit the overly long stick of menthol tar and was handing it to her while pushing the tin ashtray over to her side. 'That's alright, nothing like old things to refresh the memory.'

'I have a daughter now, she's the most delicate thing I have ever seen but she's totally fearless. Last week she climbed on top of the railing at her infant school and stood up on them, she's only small but she sure knows how to frighten the life out of you.' She thought about taking out a picture of Moira to show Chris but for some reason or other she saw a strange but all too familiar repellant flash in his eyes. As though the image was a would be crucifix to his vampirism.

'And what does your Husband do?'

'Toms a, well he has written a few things but he's had some bad luck and can't get out a block he's in. He gets a bit restless sometimes and works a few months here and there but it's not exactly Hemingway.' She regretted that straightaway, it was wrong for her to share that. Tom was a wonderful man despite his shortcomings.

'He sounds, he sounds interesting. What exactly does he write about?'

'Travel writer. He goes out to the middle of nowhere and then writes a guide. He's had a few great moments like Cambodia and Argentina but those were more then five years ago. He was writing about Norway but he couldn't get a sponsor so he changed to Bhutan.'

'Cerys, you've lived in this city a long time would you recommend moving here? Or do you think that it's overrated?'

For Cerys London was the last light, it was the outpost and the in post. It was the last place to look and the first place to find. Cerys was not certain, but she was sure that without the madness of the swirling gray city she would have died a long time ago; she believed that she might have never known it and she might still have been walking around, but death isn't always the best cure for sleeplessness. All that she valued about herself came from being in this place. Even with the Terrorism, sarcasm and sheer indifference; this was her home and she belonged. For the first time ever she belonged. 'All I know is that I've never felt so alive as when I'm walking through this city.'

But how does a dead Man make sense of that? Chris thought. 'What does that mean?'

'It means that you should have come to this city a long time ago. I think if you're alive and still willing to live, then you should move somewhere that appreciates that. The world is full of nice places and

London's far from that, but it's alive, it's challenging and everything has the potential to sink its teeth into you.'

'Would I like it?'

'I don't know Chris, once upon a time you were a young guy with a lot of weird ideas but now you're an adult with no ties. So if you look at it like that then this it's where you should be.'

'You've still got that old talk about you. You haven't changed at all.'

'But you have though, look at you. I remember when you used to rail against wearing clothes that cost more then most people make in a month but here you are dressed in Armani and wearing Gucci shoes.'

He tucked his watch under his sleeve.

'I saw that; don't be embarrassed, I think its good that you finally got over that old socialism. Maybe it was the place we lived in; docks and factories, the tail end of the eighties.'

'You were always more interested in that then I ever was. I was never into the whole political side of it. It was just the way it looked that's all. And besides it was easier to not make a big thing of money if you haven't got any.'

'It's sad in a way, but I guess that we all start to depend on things like that a little more with time. I mean we were a pair. But I guess those old allegiances fall apart with time.'

'Only if you let them.' He took the cigarette away and sent it to the ashtray.

She stopped at that and looked at him. 'Was it really coincidence that you found me?'
 'Yes and no, I mean I knew you were in the city but In a place this big you can walk around for ten years and not see anyone unless you're looking.'
 'How did you, how did you know?'
 'I looked you up but you weren't in the book. I didn't know that you were married otherwise I would have looked up your husbands name. But I did search a little through an internet site.'
 'I don't know if I'm glad about that, but it is good that you thought about it.'
 'Cerys, why, why didn't.'
 He got to the point, and it was too much for Cerys. 'Don't Chris, it's been so nice, we sat here and we talked and we laughed a little. Maybe you shouldn't ask anymore then that.'
 'But maybe I want to. It's been so long but I still want to know.'
 'Why does it still matter? There nothing either of us can do about it.'
 'How do you know, I mean there's always'
 'Always what? Reconciliation, Getting back lost time? That's for Sunday movies and cheap books, I've read too many of those to ever try and make them real. Why is there always something more? Why cant we just leave it like it is?'
 'If I had known I wouldn't have even tried. If I had of known I wouldn't be here. I wouldn't be anywhere near.'
 'What are we doing Chris?'

'I.'

Look, I've got a hundred different things to do today, I have this thing with Tom's parents in few days and there's a big thing at work that's got me tied up in knots.'

Chris looked away and returned with half a smile. 'I'll probably call you at some point as soon as I'm settled, I don't really have many friends in the city, and I'd love for someone to show me around.'

'I don't know, I'm not really much for nightspots, I am all dull and grown up.'

'As always I refuse to believe a word you say about yourself.' His smile widened.

Cerys clutched her bags and was halfway to standing.

He stretched his hand over the table a centimeter away from her thumb.

She looked down waiting for him to touch her.

'Take care' he said and moved back.

*

When Aadam William Shah Greston thought about England it was always a bad sign. He hadn't been there in twenty years, the last time he had even thought about England was five years earlier when he met a Polish Man whose Son had died on route in a refrigerated truck. The truck was due to dock in Calais and cross over.

England contained only sad times for Aadam. All of his loved ones had died there; they were survived by stone tablets over green grass in unkempt boneyards. He had left that lonely island because it had only made him angry. He took the last of his own and disappeared to America. He took her away with him.

She was only seven when they went but she was beautiful, even more beautiful then her mother Francis.
Cerys had been a baby when she left, she smiled at the plane attendants and the angry looking passport controllers at the immigration gate till they smiled back grudgingly.
But he couldn't keep her for long; Cerys grew lonely after the third year in the continental U.S. They never stayed anywhere long enough to appreciate anything, Aadam couldn't stand them, not Americans but the English ghosts that followed him around. Aadam was part English himself, he was the son a merchant seaman and an Englishwoman who fell for broken English and thick black whiskers. Aadam's mother Karen never got anything more out of the sailor except a name for her son and a hundred pounds for her trouble. Aadam never found out who the sailor was and never really cared, Liverpool was a port city, there were little bastards running all over the place.
Cerys was his sister's only daughter. Cerys's mother Francis was ten years younger then Aadam and had been a beautiful woman who fell foul of her own beauty. Francis was the daughter of a Pakistani grocer in Bradford, who had given her dark skin, black hair and not much else. Francis was often confused

for a gypsy and this confusion achieved motherhood at fifteen. Aadam had gone to see the Bradford grocer once just to confront him about his daughter's trouble only to find a fat old man with fifteen of his own children vying for attention.

It was then that Aadam gave up on Father's. He had never had much time for family; he decided that he was going to stay out of it for as long as he could. He left home at twenty five and decided never to return. Francis had married a man and he was looking after her and mother.

Cerys was still a baby at that point and the new man, Francis's letter had called him 'Riordan;' was fat and generous with his money.

Aadam was out of the way for three years having the most selfish pleasure he could conjure when he learned of the crash.

Riordian, or Tom as he liked to be known, was driving down to Kings Langley with all three of his new family in tow. Apparently, when the police found the car in a ditch upside down, the girl was asleep in a blanket, wrapped in her dead mother's arms.

The crash took care of everything, there was no more family to get in the way. The house had no other heirs and the total lack of any legal paperwork made Aadam the sole proprietor of his brother in laws property. Riordan was a lone Irishman who had come over to England for some old fashioned hell-raising but instead found himself square at the head of a family.

The only problem was little Cerys. She hardly knew Aadam. He had left when she was two and there was not a chance that he was going to even attempt raising her. He was frightened of marriage and had no intention of finding a wife just for the sake of Cerys.

While she was still in the hospital he wandered down to the local child welfare authority and put her name down for adoption. He felt foolish doing it but he knew it was the best thing for her; he had no time for children. He was as thoughtless as a child himself and besides, what kind of a hospital would give a child to a complete stranger. Especially a child that was found lying in its dead mothers arms not less then three days earlier.

It was a week before he went to the bandaged child in the cold white of the hospital. She didn't think much of him, she saw a midget under a thick hat that could have been visitor to anyone that shared the children's ward.

It took him three walks through the ward to find her and even when he did, he had reservations. She had the thick black hair that didn't belong on this particular island, no doubt it came from the foreign lands of her estranged grandfather. He often thought that when wondering about the children he would never have, "will they ever have the light hair of the people I have called my own since the beginning?" He scratched the thought and nervously approached the white bed.

'Hello.' Under his arm he had a bunch of flowers and from the stall downstairs he had grabbed a cheap

teddy bear, he had seen it in a movie once and thought it best to accommodate the gesture.
'I'm your mum's big brother, I'm Aadam.'
It was 1978 and the little girl shrunk under the covers.

But that was so long ago that it didn't really matter. Cerys was a grown woman; she had changed her hair and outgrown her once beloved liquorices. What did it matter now to the old face that Aadam saw in the mirror every morning.
Morning was inside the window now. He had been up all night and it wasn't going to be another slow day.
"She probably wont mind" he thought as the little razor scratched the stubborn hair over his throat.
The envelope had contained a photograph of a woman in a black coat. The black and white grain didn't give away much except a down turned face blurred and consumed in something immediate. He looked at the photograph and wondered why the photographer had been afraid to approach her. It was obvious that the snap was taken from a moving car. The photographer was doing his best to not be noticed but Aadam knew; he knew right away.
Inside the brown handled bag that was far too big for a little man were the remains of an old suit hardly worn by anyone except moths and moth balls. Aadam shook out the dust and threw it over his shoulders. He hadn't touched the thing in years and it showed when the seams creaked against his shoulders.
He glanced one last time at the mirror, it gave away nothing.

23

Aadam banged on the door as hard as he could.

He had been standing outside the house for at least fifteen minutes wondering what he would say to the face that he hadn't seen in over fifteen years. He thought about what he would say to the daughter that he had gained and lost, all in the same delicious instant. He thought and thought until his hands got restless and started knocking on the big black door that stood between them.

When it finally opened, the yellow light of the interior took away his sight for the flicker of an instant as he separated the shadow from the shape in front of him. 'Hello, I'm Mr Aadam Shah Greston; I'm here to see Cerys.' The face before him belonged to a wide jawed Englishman, a wide jaw on an arrogant face that knew its place in the world, rich no doubt; the outside of the big town house spelled that even to the blind.

The man in front of him smiled and asked him what this was about?

'I'm her uncle, surely she told you about me?'

'I'm sorry but I've never heard of you, are you sure you have the right address?'

'This is number 85?'

'Yes but, look, why don't you come inside and wait. Cerys will be home in a short while and if you're really who you say you are then this can all be taken care of.'

'What makes you think I'm not her uncle?' Aadam looked up trying his very best to appear menacing. 'What makes you so sure that I am not her uncle, don't I look like her? Or maybe it's my height that you're bothered with. What is it that you think I came here for Mr?'

'It's just that Cerys has never mentioned you before.' Tom lied as easily as he spoke. 'She has always said that she has no living relatives. I didn't know what to think when I got your phone call. In this day and age you can't even trust your friends let alone strangers.'

'But I'm not a stranger Mr?'

'Hubanach, Tom Hubanach.'

'Mind if I call you Tom? After all you are my little girl's husband so it's only fair that I at least get that privilege.'

Tom hated him already, the maniacal dark skinned dwarf with his shrimp eyes and oversized nose from the black outside. He came at him from the dark and now to the best of his ability, swallowed the room and all the air in it. 'Would you like me to take your coat?'

'Why would you want to do something like that? After all you've already decided that you want me to leave.'

Tom stopped, he had messed up royally. If this actually was her uncle then he was going to look like a jackass when she walked in that door arms open wide to her dear lost relative. 'I'm sorry about that, it's just that this is a little strange for me, I was under the impression that she had no family, that she was the last.' He forgot about the sleeping angel faced child under the web of black hair upstairs.

'That's alright, I understand.' Aadam was still annoyed at the indifference but he softened his tone.

'What does a man have to do to get something to drink around here?'

'Yes, would you like something to drink, but please let me take your coat first' Tom stifled the air with his change of attitude, his legs were no longer pillar like and the bulldog stance disappeared. 'What would you like?'

'Just a coffee would be fine, if you have any lemon that would be good too.'

Lemon coffee? ' Erm, alright I'll see what I can do.' Tom disappeared to the back of the house. Aadam sat down in the expensive, behemoth easy chair and let his little feet hover over the ground.

Cerys had lived through the longest day of work in weeks. The office on Cranberry had been buzzing all day. A new shipment of fresh garment ideas had floated into the workspace from New York and the Boss was buzzing with a slew of contracts that she imagined were going to come through if this initial design proved successful.

The trainee girl from Derby had managed to copy the wrong files and had handed out old documents to the floor staff. Cerys had spent the whole day trying to catch up on the lost afternoon when it was found out that the New York designs had been buried under a pile of old magazines beside the photocopier. The trainee girl had caught flak from everyone; she had been pushed into the side office and was almost in tears when her error was discovered.

Cerys hadn't had time to phone home or even do her usual lunchtime Hejira to the Trace lounge on Delaney Park. She had overloaded herself on cappuccino and worked till sunset hoping to salvage the day and the New York contract that the Cranberry house needed to stay alive. All she wanted now was to crawl under the covers of her big bed and collapse till the sunrise woke her the following day.

She stood in the hallway and glanced at the coats, Tom, Angelina, Moira and another. The usually empty hat rack had a tenant.

A gray fedora, almost childishly small sat on the highest rung. She put her hand to it and ran it through her fingers. Her hands were small but they covered the whole hat.

Underneath the hat was a tiny midget jacket with the elbows covered by leather patches. She put her hands on it and immediately the smell of tobacco flew to her nostrils.

She put down her things and slowly walked into the reception room. She looked around and listened for an unfamiliar voice but all she could hear was the Television banging on about a petrol explosion in Hertfordshire.

She looked around the corner and saw the black clouds rising on the screen; she saw the red news ticker giving away the details of some horror not so far away. The lazy chair was facing the television and whatever sat in it must have been small, she could see no head poking over the top.

She walked back into the hall way and moved silently to the kitchen. Tom was already there washing a cup.

'Who's in the living room?'

'Cerys, thank god your home. There's a deranged midget in there who's claiming to be your uncle, I tried to get him out but he seems determined to meet you.'

'Midget?' Cerys tried her very best to look surprised, she squeezed her eyes and tilted her head as though she was unaware. But she knew that she was a better over actor then actor.

'Crissy? Is that you?' the voice was behind her and as much as she wanted to pretend that it wasn't, she knew that she couldn't pretend for long.

She didn't turn round; she looked down at the floor. 'Yes Aadam it's me.'

'What I don't understand is that you said his name was Andrew?' Tom was sitting back to all of it, he threw in a question every now and again but mostly he was savoring the whole un-robing of his wife's shrouded past.

'Andrew was my grandfathers name, my mother "Karen," thought it would be a good idea to give me some kind of past so she named me after him. But I took the name Aadam after she died. I just didn't want to be known for something that never quite fitted me.'

Cerys was trying her very best to enjoy her moment, but the enthusiasm that should have been present just wasn't. 'He changed his name for Tax purposes. He had a little brother called Aadam who went to live with his father in Bradford and from there he disappeared. Everyone always thought that he went back with his father to Pakistan and never came back. Andrew took on his name after he failed to pay back ten thousand pounds in unpaid taxes.'

'Let's not drag out the past Crissy.'

'Why not? Isn't that why you're here? To make me get nostalgic about our great time together about the wonderful world we lived in? Hotel rooms and sleeping on the beach when we were broke? I remember we spent an entire summer asleep on the roof of a factory while we were in New York because you gambled the rent money away.'

'That wasn't my fault the game was rigged, there was no way I could have lost unless the game was set up.'

'So what is it that you want? Money? Food or just company?'

'I don't want anything. All I want is my family back. I want to be a part of my family again.'

'It's a little late for that don't you think! You should have thought about that in 1985 when you dumped me in a foster home and disappeared. Or don't you remember abandoning me to the state? Convenient that you think I can somehow forgive because you have forgotten.'

'I can't change the past, that was just the way it was at the time, I tried to look after you I really did. I spent a long time with you, showing you everything but in the end I could barely afford to keep you in new clothes. In the end I made the right decision even if it might have seemed like the cruelest kind. But look at you now, you have won, you have got ahead, you have a family that you can call your own; which is much more then I can ever claim.'

'Alright fine, but explain why you never wrote, explain to me why you never called? Fifteen years is hardly a weekend is it Aadam. And here you are, haunting me still, climbing out of the darkness trying to poison the air again.'

'Look, I know that I can't really make amends. I know that I have no right to expect forgiveness but I can't just die without saying sorry.'

Cerys stopped, she did not expect that. 'What do you mean, die?'

'I mean Cancer; I have no lungs left. I'm on my way out Crissy. Do you really think that I would come all this way just to see if I could upset your life? The life that I haven't interfered with since the last time we spoke? Do you think I would do that to you? You're the last of us. You're the last strand of fifty years of my life. Everyone else is dead. Without you all the dreams and memories that I have, die with me. It's not just me that would die but every trace of your mother and grandmother too. You're the last of us to live.'

'How do you even dare to come here and expect pity after what you did? How dare you assume that you can walk into my life and try to take it over just because you've found out that you have cancer? What about the rest of us are we just supposed to sit here and watch you rot away? Is that what you want from us?'

'I just came here to tell you that's all. if I knew that the only other person in the world that I care about was totally oblivious to me and the terrible mess that awaits me then I was better off hiding in the shadows,'

Cerys stopped short of him and grew angrier at his insinuation of her selfishness. 'And you think that's it do you? That you can just waltz in and out of people's lives as like some kind of horsefly? Look at me you stupid old man, what do you think would happen? What did you think would happen if you just wrote or called or gave me some kind of sign to say that you were alright, that you cared or that I wasn't alone? Why did you think that the only real solution was to run away and leave me there in that place all alone? What did you think you were doing? Did you think you were doing me some kind of favor?'

he was embarrassed, the last time he had looked at her she held all trust and love in her eyes, she was a beautiful little girl who looked up to him for everything. but here she was again older, still beautiful, but cold and with all the right reasons to feel that way. 'I cant make up for lost time, but I want to make up for the time left and if that means that I can do it by simply apologizing to you then I am glad that you're angry at me because I can make peace by argument. If I can sit here and listen to you convince me that I was wrong, if I can sit here and listen to you tell me how I lied and believe you then I know that I can die in peace.' He bit his tongue.

'Do you know that I have a baby of my own now? Do you know that I have someone else to call my own, someone else to carry on this thing of ours? But of course you wouldn't know that because you were never around, you wouldn't know that because you didn't care for that while you still had the time. It's only now that your marking the days that it matters to you, it's only now that you know because you're forced to count backwards.'

Aadam thought about asking to see the sleeping child but decided to wait for Cerys to calm down. She had that old fire that was so evident in her forbears, she had that old anger that was so much a part of all the women who came before her; it wasn't some trait that had been born just for her. 'How old is it?'

Cerys breathed heavily, she had been shouting for so long that the retort and the subject change threw her momentarily. 'She's six next year,' her voice lowered and the suspicion over the dwarf fell again. 'She's still a baby.' For a moment a terrible apparition came to her. The dwarf had come for the child he had come to wreak his curse on them, he had sensed out that he was the only living man left to call her his own. So he was here again at exactly the right time just like the last time, the time with Riordan. Five, six, seven, all good children go to heaven? She couldn't remember the rhyme. 'She's beautiful and she's got mothers thick black hair.'

'The dwarf smiled to himself, even he could sense the familiarity of the circumstances, and it was almost frightening in its regularity. He thought about his timing, he thought out the time before and how he had appeared right on the nose of Riordan's car accident,

he had appeared right on the spot at exactly the right time. What terrible thing was he waiting for now? What carcass was he going to pick the meat off now?
'Whats her name Crissy?'
'Its Moira, I named her after grandmother's sister. You remember the picture don't you?'
Aadam thought about the brown photograph that sat on his mother's dresser in the old house. He thought about the fifteen heads all in their best clothes guarded by a mother and father to the left and right of them. Karen was the youngest so she naturally got the front row of the portrait; Moira was the eldest so she stood next to her father in that faded scratch, the last print of a family that wanted nothing to do with the half breeds on the Liverpool dock. 'What ever happened to that old print, it was the only real document I had to say where we came from, can you remember Crissy? Can you remember what happened to it?'
'We lost it in Queens. we were staying over that horrible bookstore when the bailiff's came to throw us out they, booted in the door and threw our things out the window. That was the last time I saw it. It must have been spring of 1984.'
Tom was listening silently; he brooded over the image of his wife as a child, going from dingy flat to squat house, sleeping on rooftops next to the dwarf and huddling for warmth.
Strangely, he had been in New York during the summer of 1984. he had convinced his parents to take him to Disneyland that year, it was one of the few

times in his childhood that the had actually gotten something he had wanted. His father always opted for summers in Greenland and winter in Morocco. But that year they ate cheeseburgers. Minnie mouse sat on his father's knee and Ketchup leaked over his mother's new dress while she complained about the wooden picnic benches.

He was In New York for a week after Florida. His father had to oversee his 33rd investment on the River so Tom got to spend a whole week in the Toy stores and Bus stations of the world's most dangerous city; he loved every minute of it. But now his memory was scarred, he knew that whenever he dreamed about running around grand central, from now on, being chased by a Daschund; there would always be a pretty black-haired girl in rags, dragged by a dwarf across marble floors.

Aadam and Cerys carried on with their talk

Cerys was still upset that Aadam had decided to turn up but the day she had seen had left her bruised, it was only a short hour that took away her energy, after that her anger was a soft tone of short words. 'So what have you been doing for the last decade and a half? Are you going to explain where it is that you've been or am I just supposed to guess?'

'Well that is a long story. I know that it's quite a shock to see me just like this but I can say that I have done quite a lot in the way of living.'

He was coming to the point now, Cerys could tell that he was going to start a story or something along those lines. She hadn't forgotten that he was arch pickpocket of old, she hadn't forgotten that he was the old dog of the past, he could smell money from a mile away, and there was no doubt in her mind that one of the reasons that he had come back from where he was hiding was because he had learned that she had married a man of wealth.

'I've spent the Last twenty years trying to un-plant myself. I have sat around with men in every kind of costume. I've seen the world and it isn't that nice. But for the last year I've been in France.'

'And what were you doing in France?'

'I washed dishes for a month in a seafood place through the winter. The restaurant manager was very kind he let me sleep there and I could eat as much as I wanted. When the weather changed I returned to pan handling. The French weather is quite beautiful; you should see it sometime, it's really something to sleep out in the open in France.'

He was an old man that still hadn't changed, he was always ready to lie down in the street or sleep on a rubber mattress.

' I have been trying to get a book ready , I even had an old typewriter at one point but the ribbons ran dry and I had to give it away, you know how much ink costs? Those old machines have lost there luster everything is computeralised now.'

Tom perked up but Cerys gave him the "don't believe a word he's saying look." Aadam had never been much for books unless he was using them for firewood. 'So if you have been on the street for the last six months, how did you manage to get enough money together to cross the channel? The last time I checked Euro-star weren't giving away free tickets to the homeless.'

'Well you wont believe it, but a man my age still has some abilities. I met a lady on the Rue Delon in Paris, she was a big fat woman with a little dog curled up on her forearm, she had one of those little hats on that stewardesses used to wear. I was sitting down with my back to a wall and my feet stretched out on the pavement. My back hurt so I had it pressed up against the brickwork. I saw her coming and tried my very best to move my legs out of the way but I couldn't because they had fallen asleep. So over this woman comes, so consumed by her little coiffure dog that she doesn't realize that she has driven her stiletto heel right into my foot; straight through it. She walked on five paces before she turned and looked at the gathering pool of blood. I heard the crunch and I saw her walk off but I was so hung over that it took me the best part of a minute to register what had happened. When I started wailing a crowd gathered, she was still watching from five paces away, when an old man made sense of my gibberish and started cursing the rich woman for her negligence. Anyway the old woman was quite frightened, so she called me an ambulance and took care of the injury. She felt so bad about it that she offered me some money to get cleaned up and directed me to a homeless shelter that she sometimes gave donations to. The volunteers at the shelter were having a quiet month since it was the summer and there were plenty of beds. It was there that the doctor told me about the cancer. I could have gone out and drank myself stupid but instead I stayed off the wine for a couple of months. I stuck around and managed to get back on my feet. If it wasn't for that old woman I would still be lying there with six months of beard and shit stains on my pants. I got back on my feet and returned to the bus stations where I managed to get into my old uniform, I lifted four hundred wallets last month and got together enough money to come and see you.'

Tom was amazed, but after tonight who wouldn't be amazed. His high talking, all powerful wife's last known relative was a cheap circus dwarf with a penchant for petty larceny. It was the last thing he had expected but the first thing he had seen when the Dwarf entered the room.

24

It was a better day then most and the river Thames stood still. The bridges that cut over it were empty. The roar of the traffic had dimmed for a minute as two men who had only ever spoken once managed to see each other crossing the street.

'Tom? Tom Hubanach. Fancy seeing you out here?'

'Phillip right? Phillip Rowley, I remember we spoke at the Cheltenham about a month ago. Didn't think I would see you again, how have you been?'

'Not bad, not bad at all? Say are you busy right now; it's just that I was heading over toward that pub over there, I just managed to foul up a big account and my boss has just got the news. So it looks like my day is down the tubes.'

Tom didn't have time to come up with some great elaboration, he had been stuck in the house for two weeks, he had confined himself in his room determined to at least push out thirty pages of writing but so far he had only gotten five and that with out one scratch of editing. He was living the lazy dream and he was heading out anywhere that was away from a keyboard and screen. 'I was heading across the bridge to see if I could get hold of a new set of pens and there's a library that I haven't been in for a couple of months, I wanted to see if they had anything worth checking out.'

'If you're busy that's alright, I could maybe catch you another time.'

'No, no please lets, it's been a few days since I got out of the house I've been trying to get a project off the ground and I'm a little worked up. What was the name of the pub you were heading towards?'

'From here it looks like it's called the 'ring o bells.'

'The ring o bells it is then.'

The pub was an old haunt, it had probably sat on the same spot for at least a hundred years, it still had the old carvings on the wall and the gate outside was built for carriages not cars.

'So Phil, what have you been doing these last six months? How is the debt collections business going? It was debt collecting right?'

'There is a branch of the firm that deals in collections but thankfully I'm not part of it. But lately I've been venturing into something new, something with more of a human face. Events management.'

'Tom don't tell me your organizing weddings and social club dinners, I can't imagine you standing around with an ear-piece and a radio directing the seating at a Policeman's ball.'

Phil laughed a little, his darting eyes were still as nervous as they had always been. 'No, nothing like that, I deal with the arrangements, I have an on site coordinator to deal with the actual event. I just organize from a distance. I set up the invitations and the venue; I make bookings and take care of the costs. I work two weekends a month and earn twice as much as I was making before.'

'But isn't there a season for that kind of thing? I always thought that events management is mostly a summer industry. It must be awful hard to find work in the winter?'

'Are you mad? The winter calendar is even busier then the summer. You can't get away from it. Why I already have fourteen winter bookings and it's just turned towards October.'

'It sounds as though you have stumbled on a gold mine, I'm glad to hear it, but if your only working two weekends a month then what are you doing with the rest of your time?'

For a while I kept my old job. I used the time to gather up enough money to move down to the city. And after that I put some money on the stock market. That hasn't been as successful as I thought it would be but my broker assures me that it will turn around.'

Their drinks arrived; the bartender was kind enough to bring them over to the table.

'What about that friend of yours, what was her name again?'

'Sarah, Sarah Leanne, oh I called her once but she was busy and I didn't really get much of a chance to, anyway that's just something momentary; you cant win them all I guess.'

Tom thought for a moment, ten years the stranger had said. he had voiced it so passionately so clearly that his life was empty and cold without her but here he was six months later treating that same set of thoughts with disdain. Tom knew that it happened everyday, people fell out of favor but if what Phillip was saying was true then he had managed to work out ten years in a matter of months.

'Anyway I met someone new, I met a lady in Oakham in Leicestershire, I was up there about two months ago and I bumped into her by mistake, I was looking for the previous owner of the house she was living in and we got talking. I managed to charm her and now she won't stop calling me.'

'That's great news Phillip, the last time we spoke you were really upset and detached. I mean I had never met you before and knew nothing about you, but still I could see that you were very taken with this old thought of, what was her name again?

'Sarah Louise.'

That's right, Sarah Louise. I thought you were talking a little wildly but I didn't want to offend, so I didn't say anything. I just let you talk away at me.'

'Stop with that already! How have you been anyway? Did you ever manage to finish that book?'

He had hardly started it; he had been screwing out the blank spaces from the printer for weeks if not months. The Bhutan was going to have to wait for its latest addition in the travel guides section. 'It's getting there but it's becoming a time consumer. Normally I devote a month or so to research and then I give the book six weeks. It's quite organized mostly, except lately I've been distracted by a lot of different things.'

'Don't tell me you're having trouble at home Tom?'

'Nothing like that! Its just I think that Cerys, remember my wife Cerys; I think she is a little frustrated. She works full time and lately she has been stuck in the office for weeks on end. She spends her weekends and evenings caught in front of a screen and whenever she comes home she is on the verge of collapse, while I'm upstairs fighting with the word-processor. But that's not the half of it. Cerys has an uncle that she neglected to tell me about. This man, his names Aadam with two A's, sits around all day taking photographs. He's managed to get hold of one Cerys's old cameras and he sits by the window snapping away at passing strangers. The damn thing hardly leaves his face except when he's eating and he can eat; He runs through the fridge like an army of ants.'

Phillip laughed to himself. 'That sounds about right.'

'What sounds about right?'

'The, the estranged relative turning up unannounced.' He was quick. ' A couple of years ago I ended up on the floor of my Aunt Ginia's House for a month, she was too sweet to just tell me to get out but that didn't stop her children from treating me like the vagrant who had taken over their alleyway. Once I even caught her eldest pissing into one my open bottles of beer. I slapped him around and left.'

Tom giggled 'I'm sorry, its just that this dwarf is really getting on my nerves, he flicks through every channel fifteen times before he settles on something. He eats everything in the fridge worth eating and he drags himself along into every private moment I have with my wife and worst of all, my daughter loves him; she's crazy about Rumplestiltskin.'

'Is he turning straw into gold?'

'No but he drives a damn hard bargain. Cerys won't throw him out. I asked her last night about when he was going but she just looked at me with her cool green eyes as though I was asking to liquidate the local children's ward. I've never had her look at me with total disgust.'

'Why is she so hung up on this old uncle?'

'Well he's given her the old I'm dying routine, which I can guarantee is some kind of put on, because he walks around as though he has all the time in the world. I've been around cancer patients, my uncle Astor had cancer of the mouth, and for him every moment was like the last, he turned his whole life around towards the end. He quit fighting and screaming, he started to get his faith back, became much more generous and he even told us all that we were his greatest possessions, and we were all he would miss about being alive.'

'Maybe her uncles just a stubborn old fart, there are plenty of those around.'

'You could be right, I mean whats to stop him from getting a little more pleasant with the passage of time. But right now he bugs the hell out me. It's just that he is so strange looking and he speaks as though he is in competition with everyone. Maybe it's just because he is so short that he thinks he has to compensate by winning every conversation he gets into.'

'That's pretty funny, what does he do, this uncle of hers.'

'well I'm not quite sure but from what I can tell he's a French vagrant, he goes from place to place sleeping whenever he gets tired, some of the things he says are less then half truths and the rest are just plain false. But my biggest concern is that he's in the house alone with all of our stuff. I doubt that he's above petty theft and I doubt it will take him long to find a fence or a pawn broker. So I'm just waiting for him to put a foot wrong.'

The clock ticked over to the lunch hour, the pub wasn't going to fill any time soon but the way the bartender started to move you would have thought he was expecting a wedding party.

'I have been wondering about something Tom, the last time we spoke you mentioned that you were once a secretarial assistant. Do you ever consider going back to it?'

'No, I disliked every day of that job, the only reason I did it was because I kept getting told everywhere I went that I would need to get some kind of experience after university but it turns out that I didn't need it in the end. I decided to just write. One of the funniest things is that I don't really make ends meet with my writing but I still manage to stay ahead. Cerys has been a big help there. She keeps us ahead on payments and bills and I get to live everyday without going mad. She likes her job and I like mine.'

'How long have you been doing this Tom?'

'Writing? About a year and a half, before that I was working on a project boat, I spent about a year trying to build a small fishing boat down on the dock, but that collapsed when I lost interest. Before that I took up carpentry.'

'So you're saying that you haven't really worked for anyone in years? How do you get by, I mean if that was me just living on hobbies?'

'Their not hobbies their business opportunities, the carpentry was a joint partnership with a friend who wanted to open a small workshop for craft items. It fell through because we lost our assets in a takeover bid.'

But how do you pay for all this, I mean if you don't work? Do you get your wife to fund your projects? I'm genuinely interested in how a man without any income gets by drinking in the Cheltenham and spending the whole day wandering.'

Tom didn't want to get angry but he was being forced into a corner. He had given away his source, he had given away the source of his security and insecurity in one rash conversation.

'My father owns a string of buildings in the capital, he has made me the proud owner of four of them, I don't have any control over them, that's all handled by a legal firm in Knightsbridge, all I do is sign for checks that arrive in my account at the end of every quarter. I know its sounds like a deal made in heaven, but trust me its not.'

'So you have a trust fund.'

'It's not a trust fund. It's a security net, it means that I will never have to worry about failing to pay off debts, it means that no matter how bad it gets, I will always have the security of a guaranteed income four times a year.'

'And do you mind if I ask how much.'

'Actually I do, who the hell do you think you are! We talk for twenty minutes and your prying into my finances I don't have to discuss that with you.' Tom was upset, he had spent so long avoiding the obvious, and he hated the fact that that he was a thirty year old child, he detested that plain truth of it and every time he met a successful or self preserved adult it made him envious. 'My finances are not the issue, it's not as though I go around breaking into peoples houses taking their televisions because they haven't paid there license. I'm not a bully like you.'

'Now hold on Tom, I wasn't accusing you of anything, I'm not judging you for being rich, there's nothing wrong with having secure finances; in fact its admirable. So many refuse to take care of their own.'

'Look Phillip its just that I get a little annoyed when people look at me as though I'm a leech, I know that its something of a joke to be a dependant, it means that I can do what I want; I don't have a problem with it and I don't see why you should either.'

'I never said that I had a problem with it, you did Tom. You're the one who got upset when I asked. I hardly said a thing about it. It's not as though I stood up and denounced you, I just asked and you went into a tirade about it.'

'I'm sorry, its just that I always get people assuming that because I have money that I somehow owe them something, like I owe them an apology for being wealthy. Its as though people naturally assume that your helpless and they take advantage of you for that.'

'Don't fret over it. I'm sure that you're just imagining it. Its ok to be on your guard but to assume that everyone is looking down at you is unhealthy.'

'I'm sorry; it's just that Cerys uncle keeps bringing it up. He keeps wandering into my study and looking through my notes. Having the house to myself all day was a privilege. It was just me and the maid most of the day and she kept downstairs, but ever since he arrived he hangs about in the doorway watching as I type, he's fixated with the idea of a trust fund. Every time that we talk he brings it up and asks me about every detail as though he were taking notes. I sit down and go over every point and detail with him and then an hour later he comes back with some strange scenario wondering if it would make it void, like "what would happen if you defected to a communist country, or if you faked your own death for Tax purposes? Would you still get the money?" Ridiculous questions straight out of ten penny novels and European B movies.'

'He sounds like a barrel of laughs, pity I'm not around for long. I could do with a paranoid dwarf for company, I've got this dull thing tonight where I'm acting as on site coordinator at the Regent, a character like that would really liven the place up.'

'Whats the occasion?'

'Well it's a PR dinner for a large banking firm, they've asked me to coordinate the guest list and the caterers. The Managing director, one Andrew Peggot Rice is hell bent on screwing his employers out of the little dignity that they have; he has managed to request the emperor room at the Regent Hotel and the finest cuisine of the Royal Taj palace.'

'I've never heard of the Royal Taj palace, is it that new place by the Royal Opera house?'

'Well not really, it's a chicken and chip shop in Brick lane; they serve Doner kebabs and fried fish.'

Tom was silent.

'Its ok Tom, I was exactly as amused as you, I don't know what the hell Rice was thinking so I sent him a letter wondering if maybe he had gotten the address wrong, but he phones me back straight away and tells me that its the catering firm he wants for the dinner. I tried my very best to convince him differently but he wouldn't even consider it.'

'Is he trying to put you out of business? If it gets out that you fed the capitals richest bankers Kebabs and fried chicken he could ruin your whole career, not to mention your companies reputation.'

'That's what I thought, so I called head office and told them about it but they just went with Rice and decided that was how we were to set it up.'

'Anyway that's my evening, so I have a whole room of shocked faces to look forward to. Imagine the time I'll be having tonight. The richest men in the city feasting on chicken and chips out of cartons. Rice has insisted on no cutlery or plates, he wants us to use the Royal Taj Palace's own implements. Wooden forks, polystyrene boxes and cheap paper napkins.'

'How the hell are you going to pull that off? I've been in a few board rooms in my life, they're mostly pampered accountants the only time they see kebab is the rare occasion that they're on the street and walk over the remains of one on the pavement.'

'I don't know but I'm sure that Piggot Rice will find a good explanation for it, but I swear if he dumps it on the firm and the caterers I'm not going to stand for it. I'll put him straight in front of everyone.'

'Good luck Phillip you're walking into a disaster I can tell, this is some kind of practical joke or vendetta there is no way that someone would try to set up a business perk and use this out of plain curiosity, it has to be a put on.'

'Its alright, afterwards I'm heading over to Chelsea, There's a little group of people I know who are putting on a little gathering. It should be fun. There will probably be a few heads to bang up against and if I'm lucky a face or two. Are you busy later on? I have this little problem the hostess wanted me bring a friend preferably male. There's going to be an over abundance of women at this party, and its not like I'm asking you to walk in stallion like. It's just that the hostess is an obsessive numbers freak; she always likes things to be even. You only have to stay for about an hour and then you can leave. I know its short notice but you never know, you might even enjoy it.'

'I'm really busy tonight Phillip, I've got a ton of research and I have about a weeks worth of things to catch up on. And besides tonight's the only night of the week that I get to spend with Cerys without that troll of an uncle bugging us both. Besides Cerys wouldn't really take kindly to her husband wandering around Chelsea without a purpose.'

'You sound like a good little wife.'

Tom didn't like that, he hated the familiarity of it, 'I'm not kept, I'm just responsible and besides aren't you a little old for parties in Chelsea?'

'Never to young for presumption and I'm presuming that you really need to get out of that house tonight. But look, don't worry about it; I don't think any less of you for being responsible. What can a man do when he has all the time in the world to fight with? What's one little party in a lifetimes worth of fun. I'm sure that you have had your fill of good times.'

He thought about the last time he had been at any kind of social event. It was the Redferns wedding anniversary, he was surrounded by Fifty year olds and they kept grabbing his cheeks as though he were still a baby, and the only others under fifty were a few grandchildren that were as horrified to be there as Tom. By the end of it all Redfern was grinding up against his sister in law, an orange leather suitcase in a brown wig and a bad dress. And that was six months ago. It had been the sad highlight of his year. He had gone alone because Cerys was in Milan looking at a new line of work. 'I'll see what I can do, I'm not making an assurance but if I can get away then I might just come with you.'

25

'There must be some way.'

'Some way?'

'Some way that I can make this right, there is always a way there is always some kind of way.'

'You're an idiot Borowski, sometimes there isn't and even if there was why do you think I would care to know it?' Phone calls bothered Azaz; it wasn't the potential for outside listeners or the sad transparency of recording thin air, but the distance and fragmentation of actual people. Azaz had always thought of conversation as not so much the exchange of words but more as the exchange of presence, the crossing hands of people in need of human contact.

'Mr Azaz, there is always a way around a problem, all it takes is conversation.'

'You call this a conversation? You're hiding twenty miles away calling from a phone box wondering about the strength of conversation? You have messed me around one to many times. You have treated me to the worst nature of bad debtors. You haven't just ruined this situation for yourself; you have ruined it for every one who comes after you, like the man who deliberately misses the toilet bowl so the next man slips in a puddle of piss.'

'Mr Azaz don't take it from me, it's all I have.'

'Had Borowski, all you had. There is a difference.'

'Take my house; it's the only other thing I have that I value. Take my house and we will call it quits. What do you say?'

'Your house acts as excess on your business deals, Borowski your house is worthless because it's tied up in all kinds of foolish knots. Your house isn't worth anything to anyone but the auctioneer.'

'There must be something?'

'Like what? You are beginning to bore me. I know its hard and I know that you probably think that you don't deserve this but believe me when I say that "I gave you the chance," in fact I gave you lots of chances and now we are down to the inevitable.'

'Mr Azaz I always knew that you wanted full control over my cab stand but in desperation I overlooked it and now it looks as though I'm going to lose ten years of my life because you think that it's your right to push me out.'

'It's not my right, its no ones right to do anything but it's the only way that either of us is going to see a profit. What you don't see Borowski is that your sentiments are blinding you. What you can't see is that I'm doing the best for both of us. If I don't buy out your half then we are both looking at bankruptcy. We are both going to see what the inside of a debtors court looks like and my way is the only way to avoid that situation.'

'What about that mean little bastard you sent around.'

'Who, Chris?'

'Yes, the one that looks like he's been nursed by a rattlesnake.'

Azaz laughed, Chris was a miserable bastard. 'What about him?'

'Well I learned something about him.'

'What did you learn?'

'I heard that he has taken on a partner, in the shape of Rez.'

'Who's Rez?'

'Reza Ali, the junkie car thief from the marshes.'

'Are you giving me a line? Are you bullshitting me?'

'No, I wouldn't do that. Rez has opened up shop on in Wedgewood, he walked into the cab stand and I thought he was here to rob stereo's out of the parked cars. So I ran out intending to beat his brains in, he had done the same thing to me a month or so back but when I looked at him he was in brand new clothes and his watch cost more then most of the cabs. He was shooting his mouth off about a new connection. Now I don't know about these things but I do know that your friend is associating with real scum. And I don't how what that would look.'

'Look like to who?'

'The police.'

'So you're threatening me Borowski? You think that a two penny habitual liar with a stolen suit of clothes is more reliable as a witness then me? You think that by associating with loud mouth idiots you can strong arm me out of the money you owe?'

'I never said that.'

'Well that's what it sounded like. It sounded as though you were looking for a way out of this by force. I will tell you this though; if you try to use some misapplied pressure point it might just turn around on you. Pressure has a way of doing that. Like a burst water main or a gas pipe that catches the lick of a spark. It can blow up in your face.'

'You misunderstood me, what I was saying was that one of your men is associating with thieves and drug addicts, now if you're willing to trust a man without any scruples over the company he keeps then what makes you think that you can respect his judgement over anything else? Whats to stop him from forgetting where his interests really lie.'

'Your nose is getting far too long Borowski. If you want to keep it I suggest you make your decision because by the first of the month I am going to take this place by force and liquidate your assets. So you can waive it and let it remain intact, or you can ride it out till I set the debt collectors on it, who will sell it off a plank of wood at a time. Make your decision and stop wasting my time.'

26

The Queens Armor Rooms were beautiful. Aadam was definitely appreciative. His benefactors had managed to find him a room that he actually liked in the heart of the terrible city that he detested.

He had lived with his size his whole life, so anything that made him appear tiny was not new. He was so used to it that every strange look he got from bell boys and maids made no difference to him, He had seen and heard every remark too many to times to ever pay attention at this late age.

He had been in London for the best part of a week and he had stayed on Cerys sofa for five nights till his instructor directed him to plush rooms.

The notes that he had been so adamant to read hadn't proved or said anything that he hadn't already discovered, whichever half wit had compiled the dossier knew as much of Cerys as Aadam knew of the duchess of York. What is in a shoe size or a place of work? It doesn't tell you much.

Despite any anxiety that Aadam might have had over issues of loyalty evaporated when the envelope full of cash arrived.

'Tell your boss I'm grateful' he shouted to the courier who was already returning the white headphones to his ears.

He took out the money and spread it over the landscape that was his bed.

It made a change from counting coins that barely filled his upturned hat.

*

Calais was warm in April, warmer then it should have been, and warmer then Aadam deserved. It was a beautiful place once, and it still was in its way. Although Aadam had never bothered to look, it was said that you could see England if you looked hard enough, floating on the upturned toes of the ocean like an imagined cloud that might just not be there.

April had not been kind last year in Paris. The rain had washed him out of a storm drain that he had called home, so he wanted to stay away from the city and harass the English tourists that flocked to the port for beer and cigarette sojourns.

So he sat outside the market stalls with his hat in his hand reviving the old language that he hadn't spoken in years and begged a penny.

'Penny for a fallen Englishman, Penny for a fellow countryman!'

'Excuse me madam, I seem to have lost my ticket would you be spot me a pound or two for fare back to Blighty.'

The English were as laced up on holiday as they were at home. A fat drunk in a football shirt offered him a five pound note if he dropped his pants. So he obliged while a group of drunks took pictures.

A Gendarme hustled him away to an alley and read him the riot act, so he shuffled to the beach and bothered the sun bathers till the free spirited French, covered up with towels.

He had managed to make enough for beer, so he let his lesser angels take him to a café on the sidewalk.

'If you get teary eyed you might make a little more money old man.'

Aadam was proud yes, but stupid no. he carried on drinking with his eyes down.

'Maybe you should a little dance for the kiddies, Kiddies love a dwarf, especially one that looks like he's got evil in him.'

'Even a dwarf likes a moment to himself sir so if you don't mind I won't be engaging you in conversation.'

'And why's that I wonder?'

Aadam had avoided looking over at his aggressor; he knew the type, probably a stupid young man looking to impress a girlfriend by chasing out a vagrant.

'Young sir, I'm just trying to enjoy the day best I can, I've got no quarrel with you. So if you don't mind I just want to finish my beer and be on my way.'

'What makes you think I'm not enjoying the day too? What makes you think I'm not here to have a good time? I've spent a lot of money to get here. I've got my lady friend with me and were here to see beautiful Calais. But all that we can see and smell is a filthy fucking vagrant that's ruining everybody's time. So if you don't mind fucking off back to the hole that you crawled out of Runt, we would all be much obliged.'

'Fine sir, I'm not in the mood to quarrel' Aadam left his seat beer glass in hand. 'Ill be on my way sir and a good day to you too.' He flung the glass right at the mans head hoping for it to shatter and leave a shard in his filthy mouth, but it didn't. The base, heavy and round, clinked against his forehead and it was the ground that shattered the rest of it. Aadam ran as fast as he could.

The man was dazed for a moment but he caught the culprit and gave him the lashing of a lifetime.

At the end of it Aadam could barely move.

The Gendarmes took him to the nearest holding cell and gave him the bath he dearly deserved; he had stunk out the cell in the night so they hosed that down too. His French wasn't brilliant but they managed to get a few sane words out of the dwarf and in the morning burned the rest of his clothes except for the hat which he demanded.

The Gendarme's were kinder then they should have been. They gave him fresh clothes and new shoes that were a few sizes too big but good for a few hundred miles in any direction away from Calais.

Aadam hadn't had any need to keep a contact with the real world but for some reason or other he kept a postal address with a woman he had once known in Boulogne, he hadn't had any mail in at least a year. So he only ever called her if he was feeling lonely, and the chances of that happening were frequent, the only thing that kept him away was the bus fare which he could never afford.

But he was walking in that direction so he decided to bang on her door, he had a new suit of clothes on and a fresh shave; he was the cleanest he had been in a while. So if there was a time to dull his loneliness then it was now.

Marie wasn't home, she hadn't been home in at least three month's her son Robert refused to open the door more then an inch, his eyes had the hollow stare of Heroin that Aadam had seen so often. 'Robert, I wont come in if you don't want me to, but could you check your mother's dresser to see if she left anything for me?'

'Look I am really busy today; can't you come back when she's here?'

'I wont be back in Boulogne for at least a year, Robert please. It will only take a minute.' Robert's glassy eyes filled with a late night didn't want any more noise; there was a needle on the kitchen table with his name on it. The door slammed and Aadam waited five minutes for it to reopen.

'There's three letters, one's For Claudio'

'Claudio's dead; I helped to bury him a couple of months ago in Rouen.' Aadam didn't like Claudio enough to let him have the check that was probably in the letter. Claudio was probably asleep in some Tavern somewhere after slitting an old woman's throat. 'You might as well give me his mail, I'll take it to his wife, she's in Paris somewhere.'

'Fine, whatever. The other two letters are yours. So take your bundle and fuck off. Don't want to see you till next year.'

"Thank you Robert!' the door slammed but he kept on talking 'You're a man of fine character, you will go far one day.' Robert made it as far as the kitchen table.

Aadam had read the letters going down the street from Marie's, one was an invitation to a seminar on optics that had happened in Alsace two months before he received the letter. The other was in English; it was addressed to the name of Andrew Shah Greston. He thought it was the Inland Revenue so he scanned for that horrible letterhead but couldn't find it, he read on till he came to a contact number that was all long shore codes. He scratched at his empty pocket hoping for a coin to operate a phone.

Claudio's letter was an incoherent ramble of bad grammar and swear words. Someone was very angry with him but not angry enough to let him starve; there was a check for two hundred Euros' and a fresh driver's license. Never one to look pennies from heaven as a burden, Aadam wandered into the nearest bank as Claudio Tomassi and spent the night on a bed. Two nights in a row under a roof; even though one was a police station, was the best he had done all summer.

He reread the letter that was addressed to him

Dear Mr Andrew Shah Greston.

I am writing on behalf of your niece Cerys Williams Greston who was recently declared bankrupt by the Hertfordshire county court. As her only known relative

we are hereby advised to inform you that the small legal document that you left in the possession of Miss Greston has hereby been repossessed by the greater court.
If you wish to reclaim the article please get contact us at the following number

-01582-615134-224461 ext 567984

We hope to hear from you very soon

K.K BARNES

He sat on his clean bed, what document was the letter referring to?
When he had left Cerys as a ward of the state the only possession's she had were three pairs of socks and a bag full of liquorice all-sorts.
He was tempted to ring the number but he wasn't sure. There was no letterhead. Even though he hadn't been bothered by the Inland Revenue in over twenty years he knew official letters. They had big ugly headers so you couldn't confuse them with anything else. Anyone who had ever over spent on a credit card knew that.
He decided to wait till morning before he rang the number.

'Hello?'
The voice on the other side was muffled at best.

'This is Aadam, Sorry Andrew Shah Greston. I'm ringing about a letter I received about my niece's bankruptcy. I was wondering what the letter was referencing when it spoke of a certain document I could reclaim?'

The voice on the other side spent at least one minute wondering what kind of early morning prank this was. 'Yes. I'm sure we can help you with that sir. What did you say your name was again?' There was a woman in the background, but what she said too slurred to be recognizable.

'Andrew Shah Greston.'

Sir, would you be kind enough to tell me your telephone number so I can call you back in five minutes.'

'Fine but I'm warning you now, your calling France so its long distance.'

'That's fine sir, just stay by the telephone, and we will call you right back.'

*

The two hundred Euro's were down to ten. After the hotel room, a meal and a bus ticket back to Calais; there were thirteen coins in his pocket, not even enough for a beer. So he stood opposite the café where he was supposed to meet the representative that the telephone operator had advised him toward.

His pocket watch hadn't worked in months so he stopped fiddling with it and let it catch dust instead. The big clock halfway down the street read ten forty five, and the morning air couldn't lie as well as Aadam.

The time he had been given was eleven but the clock was giving him a different reading, every time he looked up ten minutes had passed till it finally read eleven thirty. The waitresses had already noticed that he had been standing for longer then was considered polite so they made eyes at him, hoping to frighten him away; his two day old clothes were dirty and ruffled. They didn't have that passing old timer look any more; they were starting to smell too. Greston was getting back the old shoe smell of an unwashed body.

It didn't look like the visitor was going to arrive anytime soon so Aadam decided to wander off, maybe he could pick a pocket while he was here, it was a little early for a good reliable drunk but you never knew. Maybe a woman with a purse left on a pram or a mans jacket on the back of a chair, it was nearly lunch time and the smell of food was definitely going to give him some regret over the waste of two hundred Euro's.

'Are you Aadam Shah Greston?'

The last time someone had spoken to him in English it had been followed by beating with a Nike trainer.

'Yes, Yes I am, and who might you be?'

'I am from the county court.'

'If you're from the county court young fella then I'm Lady Jane Gray. Buy me lunch and I'll tell you all about it.'

Aadam had loosened his belt, after he massacred French cuisine for the thousandth time. "If someone else is paying, best to get your fill" he thought to himself; after all, this time might not come again any time soon. 'So young man, since you kept your end of the bargain, it's only fair I keep mine. How can I help you?'

The young mans hazel green eyes flickered and thought about how to trap the wily old dwarf. 'Mr Greston I need your help in a little problem I have. Your niece Cerys owes a great deal of money to my employer a Mr Patrick Phillip Rowley.'

'How much does she owe?'

'Thirty five thousand pounds, sir.'

'Is it worth me asking as to how she managed to get hold of that kind of sum?'

'Its not really important sir but she was involved in a joint business venture with Mr Rowney and when the venture fell through she decided to fall of the map and relocate.'

'Fall off the map! That's a good one. I might use that one next time somebody asks me. "I've gone fallen off the map boys!" so this niece of mine, if she really is a niece of mine; Does sound like one though, what makes you think she'll pay you back? I know I bloody well wouldn't. And if she's got any of me in her, she'll be darting for the nearest exit as soon as she catches a whiff of you.'

'My client and your niece sir were involved.'

'Is that what you call it in accountant's circles nowadays? Now this is all grand you thinking you can turn up and give me twenty questions and not even tell me who in the bastard you are? It's bad enough that you got my address from somewhere, but its worse that you think that I'll roll over on someone who never did me no harm in her life. Now I'm not a discourteous old lag, since you paid for the grub and all, but I will have to politely decline whatever you're asking; I see no upside. So if you'll excuse me.'

The representative that had come with every intention of being cooperative took out a cold bundle of money and dumped it on the table. He decided that you cant out wrestle a giant and you cant out talk a dwarf. 'There are two more bundles like that at my hotel room.'

Aadam was half standing and wondered how ridiculous he would look sitting down mid-step. 'Young fella, what was your name again?'

'I never told you my name.' The legal representative with the piercing green eyes and soft brown hair looked across the table at the hideous half man he had shared the morning with.

'You look Irish so I'm going to call you Mick.'

27

It was eleven fifteen and the Westmoreland hotel entrance was deserted. Tom Had found the entrance with ease, or rather the cab driver that wouldn't shut up for what seemed like a whole hour found it with ease. Ornate angels stared down at him from the left and right. Sat down between their eagles feet, was a perched vulture of a man reading a big book from the desk that he rested his forearms upon.

'Can I help you sir.' The voice echoed across the empty open space.

Behind Tom, through the doors he had just passed, the cold of the night air was whistling in its own cage of streets and Tarmac. Inside, the warm air floated and the dust in this ancient entranceway wasn't swirling.

'Yes' he walked over to the big desk at the far end of the space. 'I'm here for the Harris hawk party. Do you know?'

'Certainly sir,' the vulture in the pressed suit already knew, 'Take the elevator to number fifteen and then walk to the end of the corridor, the Door is marked H.H.P. You can't miss it sir, it's the largest pair of double doors in that particular corridor. Could I interest you in a raffle ticket sir? We at the Westmoreland pride ourselves in charitable pursuits. This month we are raising money for Spanish bears. The prize is a weekend at the Spa rooms in Daly, for you and a partner.' The vulture man had a beautiful all contained smile, his teeth were polished and his silk skin radiated under the glare of yellow lamps.

'Which way to the elevators?' Tom had hardly been listening.
'Right and left past the Dine hall.'
Tom wandered down the narrow corridor that was hung with amber carvings and the odd wall mounted Deer here and there.
'Enjoy your stay sir.'
What Tom heard was 'Joy yoo ste sa.'

Number fifteen, when it opened, was a plain white hallway with red paint panels running parallel along the walls. It was wide and empty, silent as the reception downstairs. It ran for at least thirty yards stretching out straight ahead, brilliantly lit from above by a mixture lamps and small chandeliers. The arch of the ceiling bent and bowed here and there; the doors to the left and right of sat uneven distances apart.
He walked to the very end of the corridor staring every so often backwards to the corridor and the ever shrinking double door lift from which he had emerged. The further he went, the less and less the numbers became, he had started at fifty nine and now he was down to thirteen.
The H.H.P was still unseen. He thought back to the instructions of the vulture creature "You can't miss it sir it's the largest pair of double doors in that particular corridor." He kept walking, all the doors were single and the long corridor was about to turn softly left. He could feel the weight of the building and the height of it all crossing over in the center of this passage. He was walking on the axis, and he had a

feeling that the steel beams the structure rested on were sewn together below and around him.

He could hear something now. The steady beat of electronic devices pounded out a fire-drill of beat. Still the doors eluded him.

The corridor had not turned yet and he hadn't met anyone passing him by at opposites yet. The spy holes that sat in the doors were awash with tiny eyes. Again he was cornered by the slow thump that his ears were still immune to but his ankles trembled upon.

The light at the end of the corridor had darkened, the chandeliers had been dimmed, the lamps looked weak by themselves and the ending that should have been visible was unclear. He walked on toward a slither of light that bounced of a thin door. The crack of light betrayed the shape of a massive entrance before him. Through the sliver of light he saw purple flashes and amber swirls marching like a vehicle headlight was passing by.

He walked on and pushed through the dark.

28

'You can't do this; you can't turn up whenever you want.'

The park was far from deserted, it was full of people and soon Tom was going to be there to.

'I was just walking through.'

'And you saw me? You saw me in the middle of this six acre park that's located in the center of the largest city on this island, at the exact moment that I decide to go for a walk through it? You said yourself, three chance run-in's can't happen.'

'Alright maybe it was more then coincidence, maybe there was some pre-arrangement, maybe there is a motive. But that doesn't mean it's harmful.'

'I like the fact that you looked me up, I like the fact that you are still willing to be friends with me, and I do enjoy seeing you but this is too much. My husbands going to walk through this park in exactly ten minutes.'

Rowney laughed a little and took a small yellow rose from his pocket, it had been clipped so it would sit snug inside his gloved fist. He wore his long coat and a hat he had never cared for, a derby. 'Don't worry about,' Chris stopped with empty eyes. 'What was his name again?' the smile returned. 'Oh yes, don't worry about Tom, ten minutes is more then enough.'

Cerys pointed at his hat 'Why are you wearing a hat you have always despised, why would you do that?'

He took it off and held it by the brim between both hands and looked downward. 'I don't know? It was staring me in the face this morning so I put it on.' He dropped it to his side and looked up. 'I find that a lot, something stares me in the face and I take it onboard.'

She looked away for a moment, not quite hoping but imagining that Tom would turn the corner and appear magically from behind some ancient tree. 'It's been less then a few weeks since I saw you last and I doubt you have uncovered the meaning of life?'

'Still cagey and pretentious, I never understood that about you? Showing off al the time, you didn't even need to but still did as though you had to prove something anew, like a duelist.'

'I'm not pretentious, I just say what I think, and that's better then someone whose sentences go through the mangle before you hear them. You've changed, but not in a good way; like some might do. You often find that age softens those sharp corners but with you it's the other way round; those soft edges are sharp. We've spoken more times then we should have and I keep getting the feeling that you are trying to find something, something that might not even be there.'

Chris looked around 'There's a bench right on the other side of this little gulch, the view of the entire parks southern half can be seen from it. In my opinion it's the best I've found all day. Would you mind?'

'Fine.'

He wasn't lying, the winter had robbed the park of flowers but the gardeners hadn't gotten lazy, they had turned the soil and left a shadow of fresh earth patterned like a checkerboard running a mile across from the height of the wooden bench. The little river that ran through betrayed the glimmer of sunlight and a premonition of the coming veil of ice.

'Look at me Chris; I can't do what you're asking me to do.'

'I'm not asking you to do anything, when have I ever said anything that would make you think I would?'

'Then why do I see you every time I'm out somewhere, why do I imagine that you're standing across the street when I'm in a store or on my way to see someone? Once I saw a man walking down Cranberry row at 10 o clock in the morning and I could have sworn it was you.'

'Rest assured it wasn't.' always trivial. 'This is a popular coat, I'm sure I'm not the only one wearing it. Besides if I wanted to see you wouldn't I call first?'

Cerys shook her head 'Because you never have. Do you remember how we met?'

'We had friends that knew each other and we ended up in the same pub one day.'

'Think a little beyond that Chris.'

'Like what?'

'Like how you used to turn up at my show's or where I worked at lunch hours with some lame excuse about passing through at the exact moment that I stepped out the door.'

'Ok, maybe I do have great timing.'

'No Chris, you time things so that they appear great.'

'That's a little unfair, you're painting me as some kind of lunatic.'

'Look at me Chris, when I was twenty it was cute, I thought it was a little strange but it wasn't like it is now.'

'I get what you're saying; you want me to call first.'

'No Chris, I can't have you turning up like this, it's not fair. It's unfair to everybody. I don't know what you think you're trying to do but it's not right.'

'Not right? You think my turning up after eight years just to say hello isn't right? You think that my not bearing a grudge against you is some kind of insult, is that what you're getting at. My acceptance of your total lack of trust, or your complete abandonment of me, not just socially but financially as well. That's ok in your eyes, but me turning up in a public space is somehow unfair?'

'Lets not drag up the past is doesn't make this any easier.'

'Maybe not for you but for me, its eight years. Eight years of not knowing why? Eight long years without an answer.'

29

Between the sheets of the biggest Sunday newspaper the newsagent stocked, Cerys hid herself. Tom was opposite her on the clear winter Sunday, the first Sunday of December. It was eleven forty two in the morning and the television had been given the morning off.

The Dwarf uncle Aadam had taken Moira for a walk. She had learned quickly that the little man was practically swelling with sweets, every pocket had something and despite Cerys scolding him the thought of Moira deprived of Mans greatest achievement only set the dwarf to more daring. he filled Moira with more sugar then a sugar bowl, e numbers bounced around her blood stream and Cerys saw many future trips to the dentist for her once fruit loving little girl.

The morning solitude was desperately needed. It was hard on both of them but they managed the weekends without Angelina. Between the both of them they could control Moira, no matter how stubborn she became.

Cerys hadn't read a word of the finance ministers speech and nor did she care to; she skipped the arts section all-together and instead focused on the swelling orange forehead of the French foreign secretary.

This had been an odd winter. It had been so alike to so many others except for two things. The obvious was her uncle turning up, strangely endowed with a wealth he had never had before and the second was that vague apparition of a loss entirely her own.

Chris Rowney didn't deserve to live. Not that she wanted him dead. She just didn't want him in her life. He had been kind to her when kindness was not needed; he had tried to be so many things to her without success. It had begun when he painted her room for her and it ended when he tried to burn her down.

It wasn't fair that her past life was driven towards disrupting her present. It was unreasonable for these shadows to emerge now. These visions of a past that she had departed from, these echoes of a dream gone sour.

'You've been hiding behind that broad-sheet for an hour. If it's that good I want to read it too.'

'Sorry Tom, I was a million miles away.'

Are you okay Cerys? All week you've been unreasonably quiet. And I thought it was because you were nervous about your uncle turning up.'

'It's not that, its just work. New account, makes me nervous when I don't know who I'm dealing with.'

'That's never bothered you before. Are you sure that's all it is?'

'Well, there is one other thing.'

'What is it?'

'Last week I was out and I bumped into an old acquaintance from home.'

He hated it when she said that, because even though she vowed never to go back, she still kept the idea in her head. A home she wasn't willing to share. 'How was your friend?'

'Well, Chris is doing really well for himself. From the look of him he was healthy and happy and his clothes weren't so shabby either. The last time I saw him he was on the dole and drinking most of that.'

Tom had learned never to ask after her hometown, he had learned that if he received some strange outburst of nostalgia the best thing that he could do was to be attentive and delicate with his answers. 'So what does your friend do now?'

'I didn't really ask.' And then she just stopped, Tom waited for her to draw out some more but she returned to the paper as though the last five minutes didn't happen. Almost as though she was giving a signal to him from the comfort of a Sunday chair.

Tom returned to the article on Cambodian shrines and there use in modern vase designs.

30

The voice on the other side was angry.

'There isn't much I can do about That Mr Mill, I gave you the chance to check the merchandise on four different occasions if you were uncertain about it you should have said something. Now that you have carried it all the way to Cardiff you can't expect me to take it back and pay your transport costs? That's just unfair. If you really want me to take it back then I will but at wholesale price.'

The voice on the other side was screaming now.

'Well Mr Mill if you hadn't been so hasty then we wouldn't have this problem. If you have spent the last four days packaging and setting up a retail operation then that's your business, but I am not a retailer, I buy wholesale and there's no way that I'm planning to buy back goods that have already been processed at a processors price.'

The phone went dead.

'Mr Mill?' Azaz put the phone down. 'Gafoor, do you know who that was?'

Gafoor had been listening greedily. Whenever someone rang at Kadiz, which was rare to never, it was always bad. The last time someone rang the Kadiz phone asking for Azaz; No, it had never happened before. No one had the number; bad news traveled outward it passed through different locations.

'Apparently, The Cardiff mob got a seventy percent cut out on a product and it was only when they had gotten through half of it that they realized that the purity was under the standard. I have been dealing with them since ninety four and not once have I messed with them. They're my most loyal customers, and now they want me to buy back what I sold them at cost. They want petrol, time and labor costs. So I'm being charged thirty thousand pounds on top of what they paid me. So I'm looking at one hundred and ten thousand pounds debt.'

'Shall I get Rowney?'

'YES! I WANT YOU TO GET ROWNEY! Get him here now.'

31

At three o clock in the morning the familiar smell of linen that is warm and on the verge of going through the laundry, is all the human body wants. That was Toms only desire. He was tip toeing and biting his tongue, trying not to wake the shape that was under the warm duvet.

He had made a point of turning the clock away from the bed before he left the house so if she did wake up he wouldn't have to deal with the 'What time do you call this?' speech.

Tom had no recollection as to how he got home. He could remember nothing after 1 am. He could think of nothing.

But she was far away, somewhere clean and fantastic; she wasn't really bothered that he was making an elephant impression as he crashed around the room in the dark. He was drunk and red faced, but he was tired, so he knew it would be only right for him to get as close to her as he could and fall asleep, before the headache, that he knew was around the corner, kicked in.

The few steps that were between him and the bed became a blur; but that was alright, there was nothing beyond the odd heeled shoe that could do him serious injury if he collapsed on the floor. So he bucked up and made the steps into one leap.

He had no time to remove his clothes. He pulled at the covers till he had turned Cerys into a shivering thing on the edge of the mattress and then remembered she was there. He gave her back the duvet and carried on.

In his pocket was the phone number of a woman who he had never seen before, a tall thin brunette with paper skin and glass eyes. She was all elbows and shoulders as far as he could tell. When he looked at her he thought her face must have been yanked like a girdle to sit as it did. But she was too young for surgery. She didn't have that polished over-professionalism that male surgeons can't help but apply. Besides, she was young enough to still be considered attractive. To think of it, Tom hadn't seen any one all night that wasn't attractive in some way.

*

In the dark of the H.H.P room there were skinny blondes and loud, rich old-men everywhere; even the wall flowers that stood alone were in the caliber of goddesses.

Tom had been nursing a scotch against the back wall while all hell broke loose in riotous color around him. The telephone number of the mystery woman dropped into his spare hand, without a word being exchanged.

The H.H.P was nothing he had expected. It was a giant kaleidoscope of colors and drunkenness. Phillip was no where to be seen and the host, wherever or whatever he was, must have drowned and left his drunken pet monkey in charge because it was a near riot.

In the corner, a group of tall girls had tied a man to a chair and were throwing fruit at him like a seal. On the other wall a man wearing a tie and nothing else was being smeared with champagne by a group of angry laughing demons in feminine skin. Rowley was still nowhere to be seen.

On the dance floor fat old lizards in top hats ground against child-faced girls who led them by their big strawberry noses. The over head lights flashed incoherently as the violence of the music strangled every living thing into a submissive "Do what you want to me" pose.

At the edges shy men with ear pieces talked into their wrists as the madness unfolded.

Lying on the floor, a naked man was shooting a water pistol at the ceiling and behind him a strange looking black man exchanged glances across the hall with some other that Tom couldn't see.

The waiters, who must have had night vision threaded through it all smiling, never getting an order wrong. Even when a table got turned over by someone having too much fun, they served with greater joy.

The barmen were barely there; they threw bottles and started fires for the amusement of others. They smashed expensive bottles and threw away measuring devices. Shot pumps and mixers went in the bin as stirring spoons came together in champagne buckets of cocktails. Glasses never got empty at the bar and the dull drudgery of queuing didn't exist, you took what was offered to you and didn't bother asking what it was.

Tom finished the scotch and was on some strange concoction that warmed his gut and froze his rotten teeth to the roots, Rowley finally came over. 'I don't know what kind of party this is but all I'm saying is that I am not sticking around for the clean up.'

'So you've been enjoying the drink, Tom.' Rowley was laughing but his eyes had a nervous dart about them.

'Yes and this party sure is something, Are you going to introduce me to the host or am I supposed to stand here all night watching the show?'

'Sorry Tom, I've been so busy that I forgot all about that, come on I'll take you to meet Isabel.'

In the back of the hall, where Tom had been afraid to venture, was a raised platform with a beautiful unmarked set of chairs and a table. In the center was a Beautiful woman, not a girl like the childish faces that were everywhere, but a real woman. She sat in the center and held court with long haired well dressed gentleman and ladies that looked entirely out of place.

Tom thought he had wandered in on the Bloomsbury group at play.

'Isabel! Can I beg your attention. I'd like to introduce the young man I've been telling you about. I would like to introduce my friend Mr Thomas Hubanach.'

'Welcome back young Man, tell me Christopher where did you get to? I've been here trying to make these fools agree to the value of the common aim. But these selfish brats won't even allow me to finish. Come and sit on my side and bring this Hubanach too, I'll need a scribbler to settle this sad complaint.'

Tom had no idea what she was talking about but he went to the right of her and squeezed up against Rowley and a beautiful girl hidden behind a plume of cigarette smoke. 'Hello, I'm Tom Hubanach, and you might be?'

The plume of smoke only got bigger, as she blew thick smoke in Toms eyes.

'Careful Mr Hubanach, Lilly's a nightmare, all four letter words and angry declarations. She's been quiet all evening so I'd leave her alone.' Isabel looked at him almost daring him to drop his eyes to her breasts, she knew he wanted to, everybody did. They were beautiful breasts. Her wolfish company had been admiring all night so why should the scribbler be any different? She had found a new toy. 'Are you going to tell me what you scribble scribbler?'

'Travel books.'

'Anywhere I might like to go, or are you writing about Ibiza for the Sports-wearing horde?'

Oh no, I can't stand those 18-30 things, I couldn't write about those, there all about casual stupidity with some bad sex thrown in for measure.'

'Oh, I don't know. They seem to make enough money. I should know after all, I invented them.'

'Sorry? What did you invent?'

She looked away with the cold indifference only the beautiful can embrace 'Christopher, take him away the mans an imbecile, you let an imbecile sit at my table.' She looked at Tom amused by his confusion. 'You're lucky I'm not dressed for it or I would ask for your head. Now go back to the corner you pair of deuces.'

'It was nice meeting you Isabel.'

'Yes I'm sure it was. Now go and tell your friends you met "Isabel" and while away the hours in the dull offices you've exchanged for open fields, you pair of peasants.' Isabel returned to the all praising crowd she had around her.

As they walked away Tom wasn't sure what to think. 'Wait a minute, what just happened there?'

'Isabel is stupidly in love with you.' Rowley replied straight faced

'Sorry?'

'She's stupidly in love with you.'

'Insulting you and calling you an imbecile in front of complete strangers is her way of saying that she will kill and die for you, she'll crawl on her belly just to lie at your feet. That's very rare for her to feel that way about anyone, you should be grateful.'

'But, but she just called me a peasant and an imbecile? And why was she calling you Christopher?'

'She says I look like a sad eyed Italian who's been away from the sun to long. She says that I'm the bastard son of Columbus. She says that I'm here to pollute her Patagonia. That I'm some kind of poisoner who doesn't know why he poisons.'

Tom didn't know what to think, the most beautiful woman he had ever spoken to was in love with him and she declared her undying love by insulting him.

Crazier still, the man who had led him into this place thought he was a fifteenth century explorer. 'Are you having a prank at my expense? Please tell me now; I'm in a room full of strangers who are acting as though there at Caligula's stag night. So if this is some prank that you're pulling for my benefit, tell me now.'

Rowley considered the sentence; he weighed up the argument, and gave a well rounded answer. 'You need to do something about that.' He poured a bottle of champagne over Toms head. 'Now I'm going to the Bar, and if you move from this spot I will devise some punishment in the time it takes for me to walk five paces. So if I were you I would stay very still.'

'But you've soaked me in champagne! Look at me I'm a mess! What the hell do you think?'

Rowley had walked off; he mouthed the words "don't move" as he sauntered to the overflowing bar.

Tom kept his feet but let his head swivel, waiters rushed back and forth weaved around him, a handsome man came over and smiled at him, he put a flower into Tom's soaking button hole and walked off into the heaving mass of bodies. One of the china faced girls that towered over Tom came and rubbed his face with a tissue, then crouched down and kissed him.

Something grabbed his hand while he was distracted and an ice cube filled glass of purple filled his fingers.

'Not now Aganetha'

The tall girl looked at Rowley, with bored disgust and walked off.

Rowney was looking at Tom's feet. 'You're soaked through, come on shift your feet, there's a spare suit in the back. I'm sure it'll do for now.'

Tom followed the strange rabbit he had found in the Cheltenham.

At the very rear of the hall a huge painting of some over fed huntsman standing in a country pub while fleshy women served him mead looked downward. Beside it was a curtain that ran from the ceiling to the floor. Rowley lifted it up and disappeared. 'Are you coming, or am I going to dress the thought of you?'

Tom followed under the curtain and the blue lights of the next room almost made him fall over.

They were in a security room. The left wall was a giant fly's eyeball. Thirty screens peered around every corner and the bored looking man who sat in front of it chewed the butt of his cigarette tastelessly. 'Don't mind Jordan, he's laziest man in the universe. Follow me.'

Through a second door at the rear of the security office was a white room with nothing in it except a hat rack which sat on a plinth in the center of the room. On the hat rack hung a dark blue suit under a plastic film.

'Strip.'

'I don't think so'

'But I think you should, because you are.'

Rowley pulled a knife out of his pocket and walked towards Tom.

'What the hell do you think you're doing?'

'Stand very still. I wouldn't move if I was you.'

'Don't point that thing at me Phillip.'

Rowley jumped his next two steps and grabbed Tom by the lapel, pulling him so close he could smell his breath. 'This flower will make you sneeze for the rest of the week.' He put the blade edge under stem and tore it from the button hole.

Back in the H.H.P there was no rest, the old men had rotated. Those that were once sat were now pressed tightly to girls who were younger then the leather on the shoes they wore. The others nursed premonitions of heart attacks mid step while pretty porcelain faces laughed at their aged wind-bagging.

'This suit is beautiful and cramped.'

'Well it covers the smell of stale wine well; I can barely smell you at all.'

They looked around themselves, the fountain that he hadn't noticed before was overflowing onto the floor around it while a waiter tried to remove the wad of tissues someone had thought it funny to block it with.

'Who are these people, and where the hell have you invited me.'

'There just people like you, only a little richer and shorter on time. You might think that because they look or act this way that you might see them out on the circus or up in the square's marching in togas and walking on their hands; but the truth is that for most of them this is as good as it gets. This is the only time they are allowed to go free.'

'But most of them are pilled out of there faces. I mean look at them their zombies, their vegetables.

Their not beautiful or free, that's the façade. That's the joke.'

Rowley wasn't listening. 'Your glass is empty; I'm going to get you another.' Tom looked around at the disarray, there were things being broken at every moment, the crash and smash was constant under the black beats that settled on the strangled air.

'What do you do?' A thin delicate arm wrapped around his throat gently. 'All you're doing is staring at us? Are you afraid, is that what it is?'

He hadn't seen her face but her voice was angelic. 'I'm just a tourist, lost in here not quite sure if I want to leave yet.'

'Do you want a tour guide tourist?' she kissed him ever so gently that he wasn't even sure it would qualify under any description. 'I can let you see more then you might alone.'

He wanted to turn around and look at her desperately.

'Too late, my clocks are fast so I have to go, goodbye tourist.'

And with that she was gone. She loosened her arm from his throat, and took her scented hair away from his shoulders; removing the breasts he could feel pushing into his shoulder blades. She stepped back into the void before he could get a look.

'I see that you met Andrew.' Rowley had returned
'Who?'
'Andrew, you were just talking to him.'
'That was a she, that wasn't an Andrew.'
'You want me to call him back?'

Tom did his best to stifle his budding erection. Even though it was dark, the last thing he wanted was for Andrew or Phillip or anyone else in this Safari park to get the wrong idea.

'Here's your drink, get it down, I want to take you to meet a real dragon. You'll need balls like St George to handle this one. You think Isabel was scary, just wait.'

Rowley eyeballed the glass making sure every drop went to the right place, and from nowhere he pulled out a second glass full of an orange drink laced with every ingenious concoction a drunkard race could ever conspire toward. 'That'll get you going; and if it doesn't you're on your own.' He crooked his arm into Toms and dragged him over to a lone woman in a white dress.

'Hello Della,'

Della looked up at them and barely moved an inch.

'Are you enjoying yourself?' Rowley's over-friendliness was almost a mental health nurse parody. 'Have you had anything to eat Della, You know what happens when you don't eat don't you? You get cranky, that's right. And we don't like it when Della gets Cranky. Especially when she's in a room full of people.'

Tom looked down at the creature, her red hair fell down her face evenly and with poise. Her skin was like aged marble. She was older then the Porcelain faced children, but younger then Isabel. She didn't look up even once.

'Della, are you going to say something?'

Della's wrist stretched out like it was on an elastic band. She dug her Nails into Rowley's testicles and squeezed with such glee that her face shone like a proud mothers at the birth of her child. 'I love you Chrissy, so why don't you believe me when I say it? You came over to my house and we were together for days but you left and never called again. I didn't bother asking you because I knew you were busy. But it still hurt though so sit down.' Without loosening her grip she pulled him down to the seat opposite. 'I'm so glad that you came over today, I'm so glad that you really care enough about my opinions. It makes me happy to know that you care about me.' She looked up Blue eyes under heavy black eye liner 'And who is your friend, so coy and quiet?'

Rowley was beyond acting as host, his face was turning blue.

'I'm Tom Hubanach, and I think your going to do him some serious damage.' Della's face looked like ice and Rowley's just looked blue

'My lover loves it, how do you think we met?'

'Maybe you should let go.'

She did with a gasp and a surprising smile on her face as though she just tasted a wonderful new feeling in the pit of her stomach. 'I'll let you boys get on with your round. I've got a weeks worth of living to do this evening so I'll probably see you both again.'

Della waved as they walked away.

Rowney was still getting his breath back.

'What the hell was that about?'

'That, oh,' his breathing was a mess. 'Just a friendly hello.'

'It looked really friendly.'

'She doesn't mean anything by it.'

'I suppose your'e going to tell me that she's madly in love with me and that's just her way of expressing it.'

'No, Della was just saying hello and communicating the fact that she was very annoyed that I stood her up last week.'

Tom's eyes were getting weak, the constant repetition was hurting his head and slowly, his grasp of sound was disappearing too. Every sentence had a muffler on it and every trivial thing had to be asked twice. The color was draining out of the room and the little things weren't standing out like they once did.

'What are you talking about Tom? You sound like the narrator of a bad film, what do you mean the color's drained out of the room?'

'Did I just say that out loud? How long have I been doing that? Have I been doing it long? Have I been walking round talking out loud? Spilling what I think of the scene in front of me?' Tom was getting paranoid, all night he had been attacking his surroundings venomously. And if anyone had heard half the things he had thought he wasn't going to be very popular.

'Look over there.'

'What?'

'Do you see that man over standing in the middle of four girls waving his arms about.'

Tom looked and saw a ridiculous sight, a man in a long orange gown stood under shoulder length hair and behind round rimmed glasses, howling into the air. 'Whats he doing?'

'He has this terrible passion for poetry and Isabel has this real soft spot for lost causes. She told him one day that he would have made a Shelleyesque figure had he been born in a different time. I doubt he knew who Shelley was at the time because he was carting around a Bukowski, and thought that was some great achievement. So now whenever he comes to these little whatever they are's, he gets all Byronic and dresses up like a royal jackass; spitting out the inside of his head to anyone who'll listen. So if you're getting worried don't. Spilling his head is how that man earns his living.'

Rowney knew what was happening, it wasn't the alcohol, you could drink a bucket of it and all it would do was put you to sleep. He just worried about the dosage. It was one thing spiking a drink with watered down drugs bought in the back of a dive in Epsom but what he'd used tonight had come straight off the Calais drop, pre-sliced pre-divided, untouched and it was in the bloodstream of someone who probably couldn't spell it let alone stomach it.

'Is there somewhere I can sit down for a second? I think I have drunk too much.' The room was not on its axis anymore. Mixing drinks was a bad idea. 'Could I get some water, where, where have you gone?'

Rowney had wandered away for the best part of ten second's. The last thing he wanted was a trip to the emergency room with his new best friend.

'Phil! Where are you? I haven't even, I don't even? Where are you?'

'I'm right here, Drink this.'

'What is it?'

'Its good, trust me.'

Tom pushed it down his throat expecting it to immediately climb back out in a hot flame of orange.

'All better?' Rowney put his hand on Toms shoulder. 'Now get up, I haven't done introducing you yet.'

They went into the heaving mass that till now they had been avoiding. The crowd opened like a fold of the ocean and swallowed them both. The multi limbed animal kept on moving into the dark.

32

'Listen to me Connors. I need a favor.' Sayby was on the telephone, a rare thing, he never talked to the Slav on the phone; he knew that the Slav was a Metropolitan favorite. But here he was calling the Slav on his own telephone drawing unneeded attention to himself.

'What is it Garret?' Connors was as surprised as he could be. Sayby wasn't an idiot, even if he was a black. The Slav knew that and it wasn't going to be a long conversation.

'Meet me at the Porterhouse in Bromley at two o clock.'

Connors knew the code word, there wasn't a porterhouse in Bromley, the porterhouse club was in Poulten over on the other side of the M25 the only thing that even vaguely resembled the porterhouse in Bromley was the train Station it had the same big silver lights outside. Sayby liked the coffee and on Wednesdays and Fridays a pretty girl worked the afternoon shift in the lemon tree café. Connors knew that Sayby had his eyes on her.

The lemon tree was quiet. The trains to Leeds and Brighton had already left the station, and the afternoon in the generic little coffee shop was going to be quiet. Henry Connors was at the far table waiting. Sayby had turned up fifteen minutes in advance only to find Connors smiling in recognition of that fact.

'Coffee Garret?'

'No'

'So let's get to it. what do you want?'
'I want you to get some video footage and I want you to tail a new project of mine.'
'It's not another fucking woman is it? The last time I almost had a policeman chasing after me because he thought I was some kind of pervert and besides those society bitches attract too much attention. I can't work around them their too distracting.'
'This time it's a man, it's a man I know. I want you to follow and find out where he's going. Only this time I don't want you to sit back with binoculars I want you to follow him and make sure he knows that you are following him.'
Connors was not in the mood, he made his living by discretion, he lived in a gutted out council flat where he claimed income support and housing benefits, he worked four hours a week and put all his money into feasible assets in the names of people he could trust, and he did this all in the strength of the third person removed, according to any written documents he was still Amin Tajik, immigrant and former factory worker in Milton Keynes. Henry Connors was the name he had given himself and he didn't want to give it away to anyone after a new mantle. The sidelines such as the hookers that he ran on Wiltshire and the coke den he had on Grady close were third person controlled. He had no direct attachment to either of them but they paid him. 'Fuck you Sayby.'
'No Connors, you don't understand. You don't fuck me. I wouldn't allow you even if you could get it up. This is something that I need done, and you're the

only person right now that I can see who is up to the job. I need someone who has a clean identity and yours is clean. Henry Connors is a filthy degenerate, his name turns up everywhere. He's a pimp and an all round scum bag. If he doesn't watch his back one day someone is going to bury a knife in it. But Amin Tajik is just another face. Amin Tajik is a moral man who has been down on his luck for the last few years. No one would suspect Amin Tajik of anything. And I am sure that Amin Tajik wouldn't mind fifty thousand pounds in cash right now even before he does the job would he?'

33

Aadam had decided to stay in London for the winter; he had decided to find work and a small room. The dwarf had limped out of Tom's house and crawled into a one bedroom apartment overlooking a Taxi stand and a railway bridge. The trains and cabbies kept him up all night, but he didn't really mind. He couldn't afford the rent but he managed. His benefactors were most generous.

He picked up the phone and dialled Cery's.

Tom was down on the parade. He felt good this morning so good he was whistling to himself. He had bumped into the milkman and the grocer out in the cold and while they hunched over in the cold winter morning he strolled as though it were June.

Cerys had been asleep while he had slipped out of the warm bed, and he was out looking for something warm to wake her up with. She wouldn't be at work for another hour, so he thought about buying her some fresh bread and coffee. He wandered into the Redmond and ordered her favorite.

Sayby hated the morning air, it did him no favors, he hated this part of town, wandering around here did him no favors. The last thing he needed was the laughter of school children following him down the street but he was on orders to wait for the man to leave the house before he posted the envelope. He had to make sure that the lady of the house got the parcel and not the man.

He had sat outside with the radio for company, and he had thought about the sleepy children in the floors above him. No doubt the only faces they ever saw like him took out the trash and cleaned the dishes. Sayby couldn't get away from it. The rich always brought out the worst in him.

He saw the door open and watched the man leave, the face that left was smiling and there was a lightness to it that didn't appear right on the coldest day of December.

The dwarf was going to give a signal right after he had woken the house up with a phone call.

Azaz got out of the warm bed, the fat wife that his father had chosen for him over twenty years ago was still snoozing. Downstairs his daughter in law was rattling pots and setting fire to the stove, His son had already disappeared out the door, had to commute to the city for his big city job, blue eyed girlfriend and the little glasses of expensive brandy.

Six little children slept while the letter box rattled seventeen minutes before time. The post man was officious, he couldn't help himself, the mail drop came through the door at seven forty every morning but it was still seven twenty three when a big brown envelope decided to poke through the oak door.

Azaz didn't bother to leave his bedroom; he waited for ten minutes while he stared at the back of his fat wife's head from the doorway. She had lived in England for two decades but simple things she chose to ignore. He once bought her an exercise bike hoping that she might want to use it. She just looked at him and laughed, she was the mother of six children, that slim girlish figure was long gone, there was no way it was coming back unless he was going to pay for some surgery. Azaz settled in the doorway and stared down the deep stairwell.

The parcel had already moved from the doormat to the kitchen table. The daughter in law Noreen had decided that she was going to open it up right after she had drunk her tea. It was a big thing with a name and no address or stamp on it. It hadn't bothered her yet that it was hand delivered. She hadn't thought to read the language that she had never bothered to learn. Again, women's pride overtook them from the minute the plane landed.

Azaz wandered down with the taste of toothpaste still on his tongue, the comb had left its mark on his thinning hair and the half sculpture sat perfectly on his freshly woken head. He moved to the stairwell.

In the kitchen he sat down and grabbed the top copy from a pile of ragged newspapers. He hadn't noticed the parcel yet and neither had Noreen bothered to inform him of it.

Cerys was sitting on the sofa with tea in her hands. Her feet were bare and her ankles were embedded with dirt, she had been outside in the cold without shoes and here she was waiting for something at ten o clock in the morning on a Tuesday in December.

The house was empty; Angelina had taken Moira across the street to the Robard house to play with the

Robard children. Tom was away somewhere, he had managed to get out before she woke up at seven, she was sure that he was around somewhere because they had fallen asleep together. But that was in the back of her head. The thing that had taken away her attention was a grainy black and white image that was filling her big screen television. It wasn't the news or public service but was a revelation.

*

Aadam made the call.
He had no animosity toward Tom he even liked him to some degree. He liked his arrogance mostly but he also liked his complete lack of common sense. He loved that the fact that he was a complete invalid and that had convinced himself that his whole life revolved around Cerys. Aadam admired his stupidity.

The dwarf was going to feel a lot of guilt in the morning for destroying a good marriage, Even though Cerys didn't really care for Tom, Aadam knew that he was right for her; he was rich and reliant on her. He was easily led and the fact that you could twist and shape him into any form that you wanted was the best thing about him. Cerys had definitely found a perfect counterpoint to her bull headed nature.

The phone got to the eighth ring.
'Cerys?'
'Hello, who's this?'
'It's me Aadam. Where's Tom?'

'He must have just stepped out for a paper. Why whats happened?'

'Nothing, tell him I rang.'

Aadam waited a moment after he put the phone down.

If he didn't call Sayby in the next thirty seconds he could avoid destroying the last ten years of his niece's life, he could avoid putting a hole in the sky that crowded over Moira, he could save her from the sheer monotony of a broken home.

But he had also taken a bag full of money, money that would get him out the mess he had been in for the last five years.

'Sayby, is that you? He's out somewhere so put it through the door and rattle till she opens it.'

Tom was on his way back to the house now. He had his hands full with coffee and the baker's best bread. He wanted to go home and wake his wife gently, he knew that she only had half of today to herself and he wasn't going to drag her out of the warm bed without reason.

He strung along the lines of the ancient paving slabs and wandered to the corner of his street past a line of black cars.

Garret was walking away when he heard her feet behind him.

'Excuse me!'

He knew she was calling him but he had no mind to turn back and besides, from what he could tell from the noise of her feet she wasn't going to travel far with bare feet.

He kept on walking. In twenty minutes he was going to bang on the Slav's door. He had one more detail to farm out to the fake Henry Connors.

He walked to the black car around the corner and went for the telephone.

'Rowney? It's done.'

He put the overpriced and stupidly scaled phone down and drove off.

There was a transcript of a conversation alongside a CD in a plastic sleeve. The names on the transcript didn't really mean much to Azaz. There was only one name that he recognized and that belonged to Christopher Andrew Rowney.

Azaz stayed at the kitchen Table for another fifteen minutes reading the transcript of a conversation he could hardly believe.

At first he barely understood the topic or the intent. But he didn't stop. Over the years he had read at least four other telephone transcripts and every time he read one it had taken him at least one third's worth of reading to at least acknowledge the speech differences.

The general vibe of the recorded conversation was mostly about a shipment being rerouted from Luton to Gatwick, which was not entirely unusual. Rowney had been playing switch ever since he had taken over the imports end of Azaz's cottage industry.

The real heart of the transcript came forth on the sixth page in the third paragraph. Rowney mentioned a third act at Gatwick where there would be a "reassessment" of the goods for one hour in the Cargo lounge. The other name on the transcript was unfamiliar but Azaz was pretty sure that the CD recording in the plastic sleeve would reveal Rowney's other half.

Azaz went up stairs clutching the brown jiffy bag. He stood over the over priced Hi-fi that occupied his son's room.

'I want you to lie still' the troll voice of the blond crackled on the big screen television.

The grainy film was badly shot and the images were obviously made secretly. A man was tied to a radiator in a large room half intoxicated and naked. He was overlooked by a big blond woman and a man in a mask. He lay there with a stupid grin on face while the pair that stood unshackled poked him with the tips of their feet, his penis sat limp on his inner thigh and his hands reached up over his head crossed over by a pair of handcuffs.

The blond girl put a small vial to her nose and then raised her head back. The man kneeled down and took the tied ones penis in his hand and played with it.

The blond girl handed the vial to the masked man and sat down on the captive.

She gyrated wildly while the captive laughed away. All three of them cackled at the site of one another. And then the screen went blank.

Forked tongue.

34

'My telephone's been ringing like mad all week.'

Gafoor the fat butcher from the front of the store didn't really want to hear this. He only worked the nine hours he was allocated, he wanted to come to work, cut the shank and go home. He didn't want any more then that. Greed had been bad to everyone he had ever known. But he was away from the counter and up in the flat.

Azaz put his right hand on his hip and looked around with the bored threat of a wild elephant 'I've got people ringing left, right and centre; I've got suppliers and buyers walking away as though I've caught the pox, and my chief of operations has disappeared.'

'Why don't you try his secretary?'

'I don't like him, I don't trust him, he's too quiet. Rowney's a thinker but I've known him long enough to understand; but that boy he keeps with him, Sayby, he's a snake, he's to ambitious. I've seen him a hundred times and every time I make sure that I know what he's up to. There's just something about him I don't like.'

'Still, if you want to find out what's going on you should ask his number two. If there is anyone who might know then its Sayby.'

'Maybe your right. You might as well go downstairs, I'm sure there's someone wandering through. Go take care of it. The stores not so good while it's sitting unguarded. I've got to make a few calls. Leave your Mobile.'

The transcript had rattled him.

It wasn't often that he came up against someone so underhand.

He had learned over time that treachery was second nature in this line of work. Any one who chased money up hill wasn't going to stop just because of a fence or a rail; they were going to jump over it. That's what this looked like. Rowney was going to make the jump.

"He can't be that stupid" the fat man thought. "He can't be that?"

or maybe he could, maybe Christopher Rowney finally made amends with his old owners in the city, maybe the old time villains that had shackled and dragged him from the Mersey paradise he had made for himself, had cut a deal. The fat man imagined it from his greasy sofa and rented television.

"Cut the paki out, he's been feeding of the corpse of our old pal for two long. Too long has he had free run over that part of the world? We don't want to share with the likes of him anymore. So get him out and you can have his spot, you can have us on your side and you can have everything that's his."

It wasn't unimaginable, in a world so dense with rivalry, even an old un-remembered feud could spill over. Not like it once did though, those days were gone. The brickbats and chains were long gone, if you wanted to cut someone out you took the floor from under them, you employed a financier to chop the legs out, you employed your best negotiator to go in and take over. Maybe that's what this had been all along; maybe Rowney was the Trojan horse.

It had taken him five years but he was at his height again. When Azaz had taken him in he was at the lowest rung. He had nothing but the old Fat man had given him his chance and here he was, shiny as a new penny.

He picked up the receiver and organised a meeting with the second serpent Garret J Sayby.

35

Her house was perfect till Eleven forty four am on a beautiful winter Tuesday morning. She had a maid who was so clean it was mechanical and she had a life that was far away from the hell she had imagined It would become.

That was that, Six years and seven months of human existence worth looking back upon. She had known that it was good but it was only now as it lay gasping for air on the living room floor in the shape of a smashed overturned wide-screen television that she realised that it was gone.

Tom was gone, he had been out chasing after a newspaper and coffee, that's what she thought the new still damp stain on the carpet must have been; then he was gone. She didn't know if it was for good but she knew he was gone.

The video cassette was still playing, it had forty five minutes left and she was pretty sure that all there was left was static but it was impossible to tell, what with the television leaking glass like a broken Fish bowl.

She was seated in the silence of her house, she should have been crying, she should have been screaming; but she wasn't. She was sitting and looking over the walls and the pattern of light that had made the white appear golden.

Tom was probably heading toward Greenwich house; but that was a long way away. She didn't really want to know. As long as he was away from her it didn't matter.

Her foot was bleeding from a sliver of glass that had found her little toe accommodating and in sheer ignorance of it she didn't noticed that her carpet was growing a dark red stain. She tried her very best to keep calm in the silence of the house, even with the soft winding of the video player and the hum of the street outside.

It hadn't occurred to her that Moira was going to need picking up in thirty minutes from the nursery class she was attending, it didn't occur to her that Angelina was meant to turn up ten minutes ago with the Red peppers and mince for lunch.

It didn't even register that the telephone had rang eight consecutive times, each time reaching its sixteenth cycle before starting again.

She just wasn't paying attention.

She picked it up but didn't want to speak.'

'Hello, is Cerys there?'

It was the voice again, it was him again. 'Chris? Is that you?'

'Yes are you busy today, I thought I'd ring and see what you were doing. Is everything okay? You sound.'

'I'm alright. Are you around?'

'Yeah I'm ten minutes away?'

36

The silver fish of a Mercedes cut through the waves of interweaving traffic. The tunnel was coming up and the driver in the front seat was in no mood to get caught under the ground for the better part of an hour, with the plebeian horde that filed out of the offices and streets.

Behind the dimmed windows, under the reflective tint and the shine of polish, hid two faces wrapped in a black coat. His arm was around her and the outside world that hummed, dared not interfere with them inside the scaly silver skin of German constructors.

Her black mess of hair long and tangled, so unlike her, rubbed against his cold skin as he reacquainted himself with the scent that he had never really forgotten. She leaned in on him and her weighted shoulders crushed his arm behind her, he buried his lips in her hair and closed his eyes; he dare not move, he dare not deprive himself.

He couldn't tell if she had closed her eyes or fallen asleep in his arms. He couldn't tell if her tangle of hair had breath underneath it. He was pushed out again while she walled herself inside his coat and the dark of his chest.

The driver kept his murmurs to himself and didn't interfere. He kept his eyes forward and steered them away from the settled rumbled of a city evacuating itself at the close of day.

The silver fish glided on, but in the back the two figures barely moved. The third figure did not count, he was part of the mechanism, he was sealed in with the gears and levers. He was man as mechanism. Human flesh had the hog of the back seat; while human ingenuity and willfulness rode the front seat all the way out into the green lush of the surrounding world.

37

The garage was a dim and greasy place; it had the stockpiled remains of an ugly old car stacked in the corner and the hulking mass of a fat Pakistani man standing between the twin pits to the left and right.

The Garage had been cleared out especially for Azaz. It wasn't one of his own ventures this time; he knew that Garret would not come if there was even the hint of company. The mutual agreement of a neutral space was what they had agreed on; so that was precisely what this was.

The mechanics who usually rattled around till late at night had packed up and gone home to loud wives and louder children scrambling over steaming food on scratched up dining tables dotted around the borough.

Azaz wore the longest coat he had, not for drama or concealment just because the heater in the Five Star Sangum Garage had been broken for most of the winter. Jyoti had warned him of that, "Bring a big coat if you're planning to stay more then a couple of minutes, the office has its own heating but its got a will of its own so don't expect it to sing at your beck and call."

Azaz looked at the big expensive watch his son had bought him, it was ugly and vicious in its precision; a perfect choice for a young man in a shop full of time pieces.

Sayby was late. "Typical" Azaz thought as he returned his watch hand back to his side. He shuffled back to the wall behind him and scanned the naked girls from Tabloid newspapers, teeth blaring over perfect airbrushed nipples, faces that didn't say anything more then "fuck me and get it over with."

'Is that you Mr Azaz?'

'It's me Garret, come on in lets get in the office. Long night ahead of us.'

The Heating didn't come on for six and a half minutes, its relayed telephone temper proved true and Jyoti's chairs were no better. Azaz took the bigger suitable chair behind the scratched up grease printed desk and offered Garret the uncomfortable wood framed seat on the other side.

'At least that heaters going now.' Said the bigger man. 'Now tell me all about it. What is it that got you up at eight in the morning to post anonymous mail through my letter box?'

'You know perfectly well what it's about Azaz, and if it was meant to be anonymous I wouldn't be here right now.'

Azaz sighed and ran his fingers over the sheets of paper on the desk. 'Rowney's a good worker, I've known him for close to six years, he has always had his faults but he has never been stupid enough to get out from under. Especially not like this.'

'Well that's what I thought too. I've been with him for three years and the last thing I expected was for him to get independently minded. Mr Azaz I work for you but I was appointed to Rowney. That's my problem, I'm loyal to you but I'm bound to him. even what I'm doing right now is totally against everything I believe in but he has been acting very strange and sometimes even I don't know what's going through his head?'

'I don't care what's going through his head, all I want to know is what the fuck he is doing performing double drops with my shipments. If he's doing what I think he is doing then I would like to have a heads up. I am bound to fifteen different suppliers all over the south east and if I have a sixteenth mouth to feed; whether it's a mouse chewing at my ankle or a wolf at my ribs, I'd like to know. So tell me Sayby, what the hell is going on?'

'Alright, this is what I know. Last November, he supervised a pickup outside of Hemel Hempstead, it was an internal trade, I think it was one of your shipments from Leeds, brought in on trucks to the heart of Hertfordshire. The deal was simple; unload and reload from a truck to six vans. And that went fine I was there watching and it all went to plan except for one detail. Alongside the truck there was a small black van that also had some cargo onboard. At first I thought it was just excess, or maybe an overseer making sure there was no entanglement en route. But the funny thing was that Rowney started to unload the small black van himself, he took out fourteen packages and put them in the warehouse. So I thought "what the hell is he doing?" So I asked him and didn't really get a reply worth repeating.'

So he bullshitted you, he gave an excuse?'

'Yeah, but the worst thing was that after the vans and the trucks left he hung around the farm waiting for someone, I was in one of the vans with a new driver so I couldn't exactly stay with him to see what was happening. But when I called him after making the second drop he was in the middle of dinner with some bass voiced Irishmen.'

'But that doesn't mean much, Rowney is an Irishman, or at least that is what he always says if you press him enough.'

'Anyway I let it go, because it was the first time I had ever had him act strange around something as simple as a pickup, but it didn't leave me, not for a long time. Then it happened again. We were in Derby doing a drop, and Rowney's talking to the guy with the cash, and I've got it in my head that were there for fifty two, and that's what me and Rowney discussed all the way up the M1. And that's fine but when we get there Rowney doesn't even say anything to the guy who just hands him a suitcase. The fella doesn't even say as much as a hello when he gets in his car and disappears; he takes half the shipment and leaves the rest. I stand there looking at Rowney who just carries on as though this is perfectly normal, and then all of a sudden a big senator pulls up, one of those big ugly cars that should have been fitted with rudder and sails. This big man jumps out and I can tell straight away that this is not right. This man's got policeman written all over him. Rowney puts his skinny right hand inside the big paw and catches a bag full of money with his left, the stranger smiles and takes the trucks keys and drives off leaving us with the boat. "What the fuck are you doing Rowney" I screamed, but he just looked at me and laughed. He threw the new set of keys at me. We ditched the car at the nearest train station and spent the next three hours in cramped seating.'

Azaz wasn't as furious as Garret had expected. Sayby was expecting the stupid old man to bounce off the walls and smash a few things in recoil. But he just sat there playing with the loose sheets of paper on the desk in front of him. 'And this transcript where did you get it from?'

'I have a source.'

'Don't give me that shit, who is it?'

'Connors.'

Never heard of him. What is he? What makes him so reliable?'

'He isn't, he's a fucking thief. I wouldn't trust him as far as I could throw him. He's treacherous and cruel, but he's not an idiot. Unless he can see leverage in a situation he won't exploit it, I've used him sixteen or seventeen times and there isn't much that he wont do. But for this I trust him.'

'Did you ever ask Rowney how he got into this in the first place?'

'No, he always pretends like he sprung out fully formed.'

'Azaz laughed, 'Fully formed eh? Well let me tell you a little about our mutual friend.

'Liverpool is still an important place, it might not be on the lips of anyone who's not into Mersey-beat, but its still a big place, and there's a thousand pot holes on that dock and all of them can suck you under. Rowney is just the Alice in this particular story.

'Chris was a homeless mess; he was wandering from garbage can to garbage can when we found him. He had lost all grip of reality. He was a few bottles shy of drinking himself dead and a few brain cells away from complete paralysis. He wandered the city for a year, living off pennies and handouts. Till one day he decided to finish neatly.

So he walked into midday traffic and got hit by the biggest, ugliest, American piece of junk he had ever laid eyes on.

The fella behind the wheel was so fucking angry that he started raging and cursing in the middle of the street. screaming at this rag and blood strewn vagrant that he's crucified with the front grill of his Dodge, or whatever the hell it was.

The driver's big mouth drew a crowd and there was pandemonium. The lad in the Yank Tank got worried, all those fucking Burberry clad Scouse must have frightened the shit out of him. So he got back in the ugly car he jumped out of and tried to tail out of there. By now there were policemen and a big crowd so he didn't go anywhere. Meanwhile poor Chris was still lying there oblivious to what's going on.

Cut a long story short old Chris got out of the hospital with a big check and a bad leg. The hospital cleaned him up and the Yank Tank got turned into a cube for the local scrap metal merchants to tally up.

Chris couldn't believe his luck, he's out of the hospital a day and already he was fifteen thousand pounds up. So what does he do? He goes out on the piss with two grand in his pocket.

He pisses away fifteen hundred pound in the span of a few hours and wanders into a casino to kill his cab fare too. It's not as if he had a bed to go home to so he didn't think anything of it, but before realized what the hell was happening, he's up five thousand pound. He can't believe it. "It's a fucking miracle" he thinks, and it keeps happening. He's there for three hours and he's up nineteen thousand from the four hundred and some such he walked in with.

But by this point, Security has made him their favorite pet project. They are spying his every movement. Anyone else could have walked away with an entire roulette wheel and no one would have noticed. But Rowney had an analyst for every time he rubbed his nose.

Poor Chris had been hallucinating for weeks before the accident, the lack of food and the sheer loneliness had made him a little bit crazy so even now while he was getting a lifetimes worth of luck in the stint of a few hours; he just didn't believe enough to care.

"All on twenty eight" he shouted out and the iron faced dealer took his request knowing that he would be looking for a new job if twenty-eight came up.

But it didn't, Rowney lost it all, only to go nuts at the last moment.

He picked up the stool he was sitting on and split the table right down the center. He took the glass he was drinking from and smashed open the dealers face like a cracked mirror.

'Now I saw the security footage, that casino belonged to a friend of mine' Azaz stopped and looked and Sayby wondering if even a word had been taken in. 'I've seen people lose it before, but not like this.'

Rowney virtually disappeared. I think he genuinely went as close to psychosis as it's possible to get.
He practically tore that place apart by himself. It was four o clock in the morning and the security guards had probably been awake for hours, but that was no excuse.
He practically tore one mans arm out of its socket and as for the other; you don't even want to know what he did to him. In the end it took an entire can of mace and a stun gun to put him down.
Now I don't know what that meant, I'm not even sure what the hell it was that just went off in him but I knew that this was something that I needed.
'That casino, I don't know why I'm calling it a casino; it was more of a den. That Den belonged to a friend of mine, one Harold Palmer. Palmer had wandered north from London after an old partner of his shoved him out.
Harold was just completely blown away by the wreckage; he didn't believe it was just one man. He came in the morning and saw the mess and thought he had been raided. Even when he saw the footage on that grainy black and white screen he didn't quite believe what he was looking at. But there was one

thing that he did know; he was going to get his own back if it took him the whole of Rowney's life to get it.

Rowney was suffering minor burns and fatigue but on the General, he was alright. When he woke up, a bald man in a larger then life trench coat eating crisps, was staring at him. "You owe me you little fuck and I'm here to collect."

So Chris spent the next two years working for food at one of Palmers Den's. I didn't quite understand it myself? I always knew Harold was a bit mad but I didn't realize at the time, how mad.

I tried getting it out of Harold, why he let him live, but the old fart got cryptic; he just said 'Why kill something that's already dead?' whatever Rowney told him must have caught old Harold off guard because when I met Rowney he was running the left hand of Harold's enterprise.

It was five years into the nineties, and Liverpool was a fireball. There were fifteen major operations running through that city and Harold had six of them under his thumb. No one outside of Rowney had any idea as to how old Harold had managed to compete. Everybody knew that the old Cockney "I used to wipe the toilet seat for Reg and Ron" routine wasn't going to get you anywhere.

In the new world it was all about pissing on the opposition before they pissed on you. Credentials were a thing of the past. But old Harold, the same Harold that was the butt of every joke in the South was playing king of the mountain.

And it wasn't long before his friends, a bunch of old villains who's smoke and mirrors routine was running out of smoke, took the next train up to see their old pal.

No one really knew the ins and outs of what was going on, not even Harold. But it was a big earner and Harold was making so much money that he didn't know where half of it even came from. For Harold money was how much you had in your pocket at any given moment, money was being able to peel of a fifty from your wallet and buy the next round. He was a villain from a different world.

But Rowney had the universe sewn up. From what was known, he had managed to outbid fourteen competing firms for control of the clubs. He had managed to turn the ragged old Den that Harold where had plowed the last of his twenty thousand pound retirement fund, into a real and thriving casino, complete with bunny girls. It was quite a sight watching no-neck Scouser's get blinded by the lights.

The first time I went up there was with my boss Andy Smethwick from Wedgewood, Harry and him had been friends once and Smethwick was looking for a change of scenery.

I didn't think much of Rowney, but I was impressed by what he'd done. I'd been to Liverpool plenty of times but I never cared for it. It had its own sets, a tough bunch of bastards that didn't really want to be bothered. So we let em be.

Rowney was our way in. he opened the north to us again, after twenty years. For a long time it was no go but Rowney put the oil in the machine and got the country ticking again.

It was only when old Harold died that the problems started.

Rowney was pretty sure that he had earned his way out and wanted no more of it. As far as he was concerned his debt was paid, he had given Harold a great last run in the sun. And there wasn't much more to it but the old gang didn't want to hear that. A rumor spread that Chris Rowney had been embezzling Harold's money and that somewhere there were half a million pounds worth of stock certificates lying around.

Now everyone on the ground knew that it was bollock's, we all knew that the old timers, the old villains that we all chauffeured for were a bunch of boastful old bastards. And whenever one of them went on about something like this, nine times out of ten it was just a story, just a line to keep the conversation moving. But Harold decided to fill their ears a little before he kicked the bucket.

So Rowney got caught between Liverpool's finest who were out to carve up the old mans stake. And the Southern gentry that were out looking for fools gold. Rowney had to make a decision, walk alone around the north and wait for someone to gut him in his sleep. Or wander south and see if he could somehow make this last Millstone, that Harold had left hanging around his neck, disappear.

But it didn't quite work out that way.

The south and particularly the capital isn't some playground that you can just wander into, it's historically and politically carved into thousands of different pieces that aren't on any maps. The over zealous security services made Rowney's job hellish and the upsurge in lunatics made his job ten times harder then it already was.

After a year he had been passed around the capital so many times, by so many different firms that everyone was tired. The magic he had worked for Harold as an independent was gone. He still made money of course but never enough to shut those big yapping mouths.

And that's how I got hold of him.

He was down to last so when my Boss Smethwick retired in Spain, I inherited Chris Rowney and for the last couple of years he's been working for me.

38

The old rooms at Greenwich house got smaller every year. Tom's mother had been shifting furniture in and out of her son's childhood apartments since he had left. It was her new hobby. She was constantly searching for interior design equilibrium.

Toms Father, David Hubanach had kept his old Hobby, he wasn't going to change anything except the size of the glasses he was drinking from.

'Why don't you get a job?'

Tom wasn't in the mood; it was a bad moment for him. The bed that in childhood had been so sweet only made him nauseous with the dust. He looked over at his father who was swirling brandy at eleven fifteen in the morning.

'Are you listening to me?'

'Yes I am.'

'Why don't you give me an answer then?' he was smiling over the brim of the glass. 'Come on boy, your supposed to be good with words, so word your way out of this.'

'Its eleven fifteen and you're drunk, that's reason enough for me to not get into this conversation.'

'Are you laughing at me boy, Is that it? You think you're smart don't you? Well you're not. So give it up you invalid.'

Tom's mother had always appeared at awkward moments, she wasn't very good at stopping the conversations but she was a great distraction but this time she stayed away on purpose. 'I don't think that is the issue here father.'

'You really are an imbecile aren't you boy. The reason your wife has thrown you out is simple, but you being the idiot that you are, don't even see it. That's the problem with you and you're generation you have no opinions about anything. All you have is the morality that you don't even believe in. You're so busy trying to do the right thing that you forget to ask if it's the right thing for you.'

'The reason Cerys threw...... Look! She didn't throw me out. I left of my own accord. And I don't see how that's got anything to do with her not respecting me. So just stop it with your half cocked attempts at wisdom.'

'I never said anything about being wise, just level headed. Do you think that I'm sitting where I am because I'm wise? Do you know what happens to wise men? They end up drinking Hemlock and inspiring lunatic socialists to mass genocide. Wise! I'd rather be shrewd any day of the week. I'll leave you to be wise you spoiled rich Brat.'

Tom wanted so badly to win an argument with his father, it had felt like a thousand years since the last time old David Hubanach had nodded his head in recognition and that was only because Tom had caught a fish while his father hadn't caught anything all day, long ago in Tingrith in the spring of seventy eight. 'I've never asked you for a thing old man so don't try and pretend as though I have.'

'I know you haven't boy, you have never had gall enough to ask me. You just put your mother up to it and had her get you all the junk you desired. Do you remember the trip to Venezuela when you were fourteen? Or the Honda Valkyrie motorbike? Or best of all the Wedding I paid for with that tramp wife of yours.'

'I told you before about that Father, say what you want about me but you leave her out of it.'

'I'm, sorry but I won't acknowledge a bastard as my granddaughter even if you do.' The old man snarled because he knew Tom would never do anything about it.

'Stop it old man. Now is not the time.'

'You let that woman make a damn fool of you every day and you don't even see it, she didn't choose you because you're you, its because you're my son and she knew it. She chose you because it's me she wanted,' he smiled down into his glass 'Or my bank account at least. This is all to plan. She is getting what she wants handed to her. And you!' He looked up from his drink 'You agreed to give her fifty percent of your assets? You must have been out of your mind!'

'How do you know about that?'

'Well you did use my law firm, the law firm that I own. Did you really think I would offer them that much generosity if I didn't have some control? I was in that office the minute you stepped out. There was no way in hell I was going to let that little half breed bitch take whats mine. So I amended it. I sat down with Welby, Wretton and Willimer. Got those fat old bastards in the same room and worked out a way to keep that bitch's claws out of my assets.'

'You can't do that! I gave my word and Moira's like my own; she can have everything that belongs to me.'

'Not as long as I'm breathing boy, there's no way in hell I'm handing out the last fifty years to some two penny, ha'penny cunt that caught your eye on the Mersey. I didn't work my arse off for two lifetimes to have some outsider bitch eat me alive in old age, I won't stand for it. You brought this nobody into my house and I'll be damned if I'm laying my hat down for her. You might feel obliged to shoot yourself in the foot and keep smiling but I'm not that kind of man.'

Tom stood without a word, he knew that there was nothing he could do to reverse his fathers decision, there was no power on earth that could make the old man see differently. 'Please father, don't do this, I gave her my word, I gave her my oath. Its like you always said, a man is only as good as his word.'

'I said that? I never said that you idiot. That's some bastard proverb taken from your mother's side of the family. Why would I say something so foolish? Do you think your life is easy because I keep my word.' through brandy soaked skin the old man laughed riotously. 'You really are funny boy; tell me has she got you bagging lunches for her too?'

'Father why is it that every time I come to see you it's always the same it's always the...............'

'Come to see me? Is that what you're calling this? Turning up on my door at midday and asking for your old room, while your own house is overrun by a nobody that you stupidly fell for? You really are a bigger idiot then I ever gave you credit for Thomas!

Why can't you just see whats happened to you? Why can't you see what that bitch has done to you? You're less then zero; she's taken your pride and your dignity; she's sapped your integrity and motivation, she's left you as nothing. A drivel spouting lackey without any drive. Can you believe that you're the same boy who graduated with Honors from the best university in this entire Kingdom. That same boy whose classmates now run their own companies? Do you remember Beeston? The fat little boy that you used to drag home for Christmas because his father was a Hong Kong drunkard. He's the head of Langley Steel's South American wing. Do you know what the share portfolio for Langley is worth right now? Does it even register in your head that there are more important things in life then just plain arrogance.'

'I suppose you think money is important do you? Well it isn't.'

'Do you think it's about money boy? Do you think I ran around for forty years because of little pieces of paper? It's about winning, it's about proving that you are worth something, it is about achieving and succeeding where others fail. I don't care if you mop floors or fly jets, there has to be pride in a man otherwise he is just a slave. And that's what you are, you're a slave. You're weak, not because of anyone or anything. You're weak because it's easier to be weak, it's simpler; its what your whole stinking world has become. It's as though strength is a disgraceful thing. It's as though being right is somehow wrong it's as though winning is somehow shameful. And it's a disease that's ruining you.'

'You belong in a museum. What have you ever done for anyone other then yourself? What have you ever done for the benefit of anyone else? When have you ever been kind to anyone? You're the one who's the slave. Look at you, drunk and its not even midday! No one can stand you; they avoid you like some reptile. You're a monster and you don't even know it. You're so consumed by power and lust that you don't even see that's its left you bare. It's left you in the middle of the day in your underwear! When was the last time you went out of this house without feeling useless, when was the last time you counted for anything!'

'I've had my run boy and I've got no regrets. I've done everything I ever wanted to do and I've done it twice. There is nothing that you could ever say that would make me feel remorse. I'm damn proud of the life I've lived and I don't really care what you might think of it. I'll be dead and gone soon but you will still have to salute me through gritted teeth when you get those checks at the end of every quarter. There is no way in hell that you will ever get away from me you stupid, homeless, invalid.'

39

Marchman house belonged to the Clarke's of Dartford. It wasn't really a house at all; it was a one up one down cottage with a thatched roof and out door plumbing. The Clarke's were planning to retire here and till then they were letting it earn its keep. It was in the charge of a one Geoffrey Ford, a big friendly Sheffield man who had wandered into the lettings trade after he gave up hawking insurance to the old.

Rowney had been coming here for the past three years. It had acted as his quiet house for the first time and after that he booked it for two years solid in the middle of winter. The Clarke's had it from January to September, and even before they arrived it was easy to see that they were a real family, complete with vandal children and untrained dog. Rowney had found names scratched into the bedroom walls "Jon and Carrie was here 02" and the same for 03 and 04.

Normally Rowney would come to the Marchman and spend the week in old clothes; he would put away his suit and dig holes in the garden or pull out a book that he was never going to read. It was always something strange like a Fitzgerald. But he never finished any of them.

Mrs Clarke had been kind enough to leave them over the fireplace and the last three years had managed to bring six orphans together. There was Kesey, Salinger, Woolf, Mistry, and Wolfe and here was Fitzgerald come to join the great unread.

Cerys had gone to the kitchen; she was thirsty after the long drive. She still didn't know why she had called Chris of all people, and she didn't even know why he had brought her to Hampshire. But she was here nonetheless, in the cottage that was called Marchman.

The silver fish had left straight away. The driver had let them out and disappeared. Rowney nodded and let him leave. Cerys had thought about asking "how are we going to get back?" and then thought better of it.

The tap water came out clean and Cerys was glad of that, she had expected brown mud, she was wrong again. Rowney hadn't said anything and neither had she. They had decided not to talk, without even agreeing out loud.

Rowney had wandered out to the garden which had died in the autumn. The ground was already hard so if he felt inclined, he would have to find a pick to break the surface. His shoes were "not right" he thought. So he walked back to house past the bowl of dead flowers on the doorstep.

He had taken his phone upstairs and buried it under the shoes in the wardrobe; he had done the same with Cerys own cellular monster.

There was fresh linen in the closet; Mr Ford had been here a few days earlier to make sure it was ready. Marchman house was the only property that made any money in the winter. The other seven properties that Ford controlled were locked up till spring, even the owners kept away. Only the Clarke's kept upkeep themselves. Others preferred to farm out the work through Mr Ford.

He was sitting on the edge of the bed when she came up behind him, desperately wanting to say something. He could tell that there was another argument in her eyes; he knew what she was going to say. He could tell that she was going to say that she wanted to go home, so he pulled her toward him and laid her down on the bare mattress.

She resisted, she resisted because it was not right to repeat the past. She resisted, because ghosts are a sad site resurrected.

But he laid her down regardless. They still weren't speaking and that's how it remained till morning.

The bed was a mess of clothes. An old blanket had kept the cold from them in the night. And in the morning the curtains that they had forgotten to close betrayed them to the sunlight. He was still thin, as thin as he had always been, but she was bigger now, and he could see it.

Once upon a time he had contained her, because she was shy around him, he had held her limp and coy because she was younger and different. But now she was learned, like a different person, a different texture and a different shape.

He had forgotten that she was a mother now. He didn't remember that she had gained a child in the time that he had been gone. Her body was different. It was still strong, but worn. It had marks on it that he had never seen before.

There were bruises that she had accumulated in the time he was away. There was skin that had grown different in the time he had been away. Even the smell of her was different from the last time, before she went away.

In the half light of evening he hadn't seen it but the morning lights didn't help her hide a thing. The thin body of old had disappeared, and now there were new shapes and fields upon her. There were new lines that were not there before.

He wondered if she was thinking the same thing as he was. He wondered if she had noticed the black bruise that was on his ribcage under his right nipple. But her face was turned away; she was looking at the tiny gold band wrapped around her finger. She was thinking about the little tie that binds.

There was no food in the house. Rowney hadn't considered anything that far ahead. When the morning arrived, if it arrived; it could take care of itself.

But here it was and it was a three mile walk on a cold morning to the shop in the village. He could find butter bread and milk on the shelves at the Acreage store that had a fat, old, friendly woman behind the counter. Cerys still hadn't said a word to him nor he to her. There was still a silent thought that passed back and forth between them. It was with him till he slammed the door shut.

Cerys came down the stairs wrapped in Chris's shirt and the blanket that had kept her warm all night. She hadn't considered what would happen in the middle of a field at the end of the day. Even when she rode the silver fish out of the city it had not bothered her that she was heading outward, toward something that was avoidable if she chose to avoid it.

There was no television to flick through and forget. There was nothing in the cupboards that would let her take her mind from what had just happened. There wasn't anything that she could transfer her thoughts to; just this empty house where the dust sheets sat still and the windows kept in the stuffy taste of enclosed air. She went back upstairs to find some other distraction.

'You're awake.' He was smiling with both hands full of shopping. She didn't reply. "It was a mistake" he thought as she turned away from him, and any minute now she's going to call it what it is. 'I'll, I'll see what I can do, I'm sure you're hungry.'

She sat down on the dust sheet. She had found a cigarette in the box room, probably left behind by one of the Clarke children; Rowney had left his packet in the Silver Mercedes. She hadn't touched cigarettes, except the once, since she moved south, but she wasn't south anymore; she was in some other place.

She was dressed but the blanket still had her shoulders. "What, have I done" the voice in her head was very slow and deliberately soft. It wasn't as mocking as it should have been. She wanted it to scream at her, to rage, to make her cry. But it whispered slowly "what have I done."

Chris was scrambling eggs the best he could. He was making a mess in the kitchen but now was hardly the time to think of that. The butter splashed onto his clothes from the frying pan and the tea kettle had boiled over onto the stove. He moved his hands quickly and burned the tips of his fingers. Behind him the toast was blackening in the electric toaster, but he didn't notice. He was busy running a dusty plate under the cold tap.

When he came through from the kitchen with a sloppy mess on a plate, she was staring out the window with her cigarette next to her cheek. She had propped her elbow up onto her crossed legs in anticipation. She looked old, older then he had ever thought she could become, older then he could ever imagine. "The sun did that sometimes" he thought; it makes every line stand out like it was carved by a blunt saw. Even her hair, that black fire that sat unkempt on her head was flat and dead against her face. Her clothes had been in a pile at the end of the bed and it showed; it showed her up.

'Maybe you should eat something? Get your energy back.'

She looked at him with hell on her face "you weren't that good" she thought to herself. "And if you think it's going to happen again your wrong so get it out of your head." She didn't need to say it out loud.

'Look, Cerys. I'm glad you came I have been thinking about you and.'

She looked at him with dead eyes, waiting for him to say something, anything.

He wimped out. 'Its, its good that were talking again.'

She returned to her window, nodding her head, the cigarette was almost gone.

He pushed the plate toward her, 'Try some of the food. I made them just how you like them. I remembered.'

She looked at the burnt toast and pile of rubbery dry eggs, the tea was spot on, weak as dishwater. She wanted to smile but she couldn't bring herself to do it.

He sat opposite her and tried to look her in the eye before she looked away again. 'Are you not even going to?'

'Speak? Is that what you want me to do?' A low rumble, a clear low rumble washed over the space between them. It was a voice he had never heard before, or the voice he had trained himself to forget. 'Well, go ahead and tell me what we could possibly talk about?'

'Last night.'

'That was a stupid mistake, I was upset and I didn't know what I was doing, so I didn't decide; I just let it happen.'

'Are you saying that I? Is that what you're trying to say to me?'

She stopped talking.

'Say it if you want to say it. But there was nothing forced about it. We made love like we always have and you were there with me the whole time.' He put his hand out to her face to maybe turn her head. She flinched back. 'I'm not talking to my self here Cerys!' His voice had gotten louder, he wasn't shouting but that was definitely coming.

She got up and threw the remains of the cigarette in the center of the scrambled eggs.

'Where are you going?' he was upset, so he reached out to grab her wrist. But she was too quick for him. 'Where are you going?'

She walked to the stairwell and went up again. Her bare feet, as she turned the corner, was the last he saw of her till late afternoon,.

He cleaned up the mess he had made in the kitchen and went out to the garden. He could have killed for a cigarette but all he got was the vapors she had left behind.

Cerys stayed upstairs all afternoon. She was stranded here in Hampshire. She had nowhere left to go. The Marchman house was her improbable home, till whatever was happening in her life returned to normality. She knew it was false hope but she had to cling to something.

Mrs Clarke hadn't changed a thing, not a single shovel was out of place; not a pick sat rusted or crooked. Rowney lifted the heaviest handled pick he could see and returned to the garden that was gray, brown; waiting for the weather to kill it in old age.

He smashed the sharp end and cracked the shell of the surface, underneath the grey death sat more of the same. The cold had already worked into the first few inches, and was only going to go deeper in the next few months till it froze the earth solid. Rowney smashed away regardless, attacking some impotence that had to be defeated. He crashed away at the ground that he had to share the week with. He scratched away the cold gray till he could see something softer, till he could turn over the ground revealing the sight of the ripe earth underneath. The scratches he had made gave out a stony crop and he crucified a worm that left a trail of blood across the floor.

He carried on till he was he was at the center of a turned over piece of earth, only where he stood remained the same. He carried on till his hands revealed the welts of a new skin. The sweat gathered and his hands slipped over the wooden handle, his sweat was dark and red. It stained the wood but he wasn't paying attention.

His hands had been away for too long and now he was paying for the weak year he had lived, pushing paper was no longer the right way to live and he knew it. Counting money was not meant for men. And this was where that was proven.

He thought he felt eyes from the upstairs window watch him but she wasn't, she was somewhere else altogether.

40

'Thomas you should telephone her, tell her your side. There is always a way out of this kind of thing, it's a hard way but there is always a way.'

He didn't want advice especially not from his mother; she was hardly the person to ask. She hadn't had to make a real decision in fifty years. Father had made sure that she was his own personal invalid, totally reliant on him and the power he wielded. 'I really don't want to talk about it mum, if you don't mind. I just want to sit down and get it out of my head for long enough to get right. If I sit here and try to make sense of it I'll just upset myself further. So please just let me deal with it in my own way.'

'Have you called her yet?'

'Her phones on but she isn't answering.'

'Has she got Moira with her?'

'I don't know, I think so.'

'Well are you going to go round to the house or are you going to lie on your belly right here and not move?'

'That sounds about right. I think I'm going to do that. So if you don't mind.' She wasn't taking the hint.

'I think you should go round and talk to her.'

'That's just not the right thing to do, she can't stand the sight of me and.'

'And you still haven't told us what it was that's made you turn up here cap in hand?'

'It's a long story mother you don't really want to?'

'Its not as if you're going anywhere and neither am I.'

'I'd rather not get into it with you mother, it's complicated?'

'Try me.'

'I don't know if I should.'

'If you don't talk about it how are you ever going to talk to her about it?' She was glad she had taken that counseling course last spring.

He could tell that that community college courses were in full effect. 'I made a stupid mistake, which I didn't think would come back at me.'

'Was it another?'

'Yes it was'

'It seems it's a trait then.'

'I never did anything like that before, it was just a certain time and a certain place, and I don't know what happened I just didn't think she would ever find out and she did and know I'm asleep here in my old room while she?' he stopped and almost let a tear fall, but then turned away instead. 'I have no idea whats going on and I've cut myself out.'

'You're not the first man in the world to ever destroy a marriage and you wont be the last, I can tell you that much. But beside that simple fact is the other; which is that you can't live with someone for as long as you have and pretend as though it doesn't matter.' she couldn't remember how long but she knew it had been a long time. 'You can't stay with someone and then throw it all away for the sake of pride. Anger and jealousy are powerful but they don't last long. After they go away there's only loneliness. And even though Cerys is probably far from longing after you, it doesn't mean that she's in the right mind to decide whats happening next. It means that you still have a chance to fix this.'

He wanted to believe her so much, he wanted to feel five again just so his mother would be right; just like when she told him about why snow falls or cows walk on four legs. He wanted her to be right not just for him but for everyone who had ever let regret become their only function. 'I want to believe you but I've been alive for far too long.'

'No you haven't, you haven't even seen half of it, you're closer to optimism then I could ever be. So don't get sad and don't turn the page on it just because you messed up for the first time. If she really cares and it's apparent that you do too, then you will both sit down, hopefully without lawyers or friends to guide and push you; you'll both sit down and work this out. Because you can't throw away and start afresh every time; you can't because you don't have the stamina for it. You lose that power after time and you can't get it back. Reinvention is a vice for children not adults.'

'I remember when I first brought her here, she was really worried that she'd do something wrong or say something crude. She was afraid that she might upset you, or misunderstand you and all I could think of was "God please don't let them say anything bad about her, please don't let them embarrass themselves and me." He smiled to himself.

'I remember that day, we had duck and Chinese noodles because dinner burned in the new oven. We were sitting at the grand table eating take out and she was smiling because she thought it strange. We had all dressed up for The Red dragon's finest noodles.'

'Dad didn't like her though, he thought she was common.'

'Your father doesn't like anyone, the only people he likes are those that he chooses to like and even that doesn't last. Do you know what he said to my father on the night before our wedding? He said "Leopold, your daughter is a wonderful woman but don't expect me to change my habits for her." Your grandfather was amazed. I mean what kind of a son in law would say that? What kind of man would have the nerve to tell his father in law something like that?'

'And did he?'

'Did he what?'

'Change his habits?'

She didn't know how to answer that, it was painful to talk about things that she had consciously avoided for years; but her son was a wreck. 'No he didn't, and he still hasn't. He's an old man now but he is still David Hubanach in every single way.'

Tom knew, he had even seen it a few times, he remembered one New Years Eve when he was back from school for the holidays and his father took him to a party on the roof of a hotel in Brighton. The weather was cold enough to stain the ground with ice and the ladies, foolhardy enough to wear heels, paid dearly every time they landed on their arses. But his father was dancing in the middle of the ice with a woman taller then himself and he was smiling in a way that

Tom had never seen him smile. He was happy where he was; on a ledge, freezing but not alone. He almost shared the memory with his mother but it would have been cruel to let her know that she would never have her own husband look at her that way. 'What a strange thing it is to see, feel and hurt.'

'There isn't much else that matches it; there isn't much else in the world that's more interesting. Your father always talks about money and security, but even he would know what I mean.'

'Why did you stay all this time? What was it that made you stay, even after all the shit, the lies and coldness; why did you stay?' He knew it would be the maternal excuse he had a feeling that she would say the obvious.

'For myself.' In the flattest tone she could manage. 'I stayed for myself. I didn't stay for him or you or anyone. I stayed because this is mine, all of it. I don't belong but it belongs to me, and I wasn't about to give it away to anyone else. I refused to share it with anyone. This is my life and I have been here watching it from the beginning. Once I remember finding a picture of him with some woman, a beautiful woman on a ski slope somewhere far away and I didn't know what to do about it. So I decided to burn all his files. I went into his study and emptied his cabinet onto the floor and set fire to it right there and then. I was so angry that I didn't even think that the smoke would kill me. I didn't even think that the fire would spread. I just did it because I needed to get some kind of recognition. I wanted him to know that I was still here,

I hadn't disappeared into the attic or the cellar like an old hobby horse.'

'What did he have to say about it?'

'Nothing, he was angry enough to smash a few things and spend the night away in a bar somewhere on the other side of the city. But he was never foolish enough to leave his trophies lying around again. I knew about them, all of them. every time I went away the staff would tell me about Sir's guests; So I wasn't completely blind to it, but I wasn't about to give it all away to someone who didn't earn it. I wasn't that weak. I picked it, even though it was painful to know that I would never have a real husband. If I tried, I could gain a family and a home and a life that's mine alone. Do you think he could cope if I left? Do you think he would last five minutes without me? Do you think the hogs he feeds would care if he was starving or alone? No Tom, and even though he is a ridiculous bull headed old fool, he knows that he needs me a whole lot more then I need him.'

41

Rowney had managed to get the fire burning, Mr Ford had left a pile of firewood out in the shed and the can of petrol that sat next to it kept the house warm on the second night.

Cerys had come down from the upstairs room she had sat in all day.

Rowney's hands were red and burning from the earth he had dug earlier, he could hold a mug in them and not much else. Cerys didn't really want to look at him but in the cramped space it was impossible not to.

'Do you remember Derek, the old black man? He used to live in the flat below us.'

She looked at him, her face said bored and uninterested. She knew who he was talking about though.

'Well Derek died the winter after you left. He must have taken a shine to you because he left you his lamp, he always asked about you even after you left. I didn't really tell anyone that you had gone for good so people would ask me to pass on their hello's over the phone.'

She was listening but she was imitating a distracted insomniac that she had once seen on the television.

'Derek left you his lamp the one you said looked like a dead fish standing on its tail? He left it to you, His son came upstairs and gave it to me the week they were clearing his flat, can you believe that, he left everything else to the local charity shop but he gave you his lamp because you always told him how ugly it was.'

'I never said it was ugly, I said it was obscene.'
'Same thing, well that's what I think anyway. It wasn't the same after you went people who I had nothing akin to, started dropping by asking after you and I made a whole bunch of acquaintances. Do you remember Connie the girl who worked in the off license? she did your hair once and pretty much ruined it for a week. Well we went out a few times after you left, nothing ever came of it because I was distracted but it was strange because when you were around I always had the feeling that she didn't like me.'
'No one disliked you Chris, they just thought you were too polite that's all, it put them off, they didn't know how to act around you.'
'Me, polite?'
'Yes, don't you realize that about yourself? Sometimes it's painful to watch. I remember that it used to drive me mad when you stopped mid sentence and excused yourself for sniffing you nose. Or better yet, rubbing the fluff of your clothes while I was trying to tell you about oppressive regimes in the Far East.'
'I remember that, when we first met, you used to go on anti nazi marches and socialist protest walks, I never understood that about you, I mean you were kind of secretive and self contained but you had this massive heart and wanted to give everything of yourself to everyone. It always confused me.'
'Not anymore, I've downsized my humanitarian efforts to a direct debit payment to Oxfam at the end

of the month. Or maybe a copper coin in a musicians case on the tube.'

'What a time it was to be alive.'

'It was only a few years ago Chris?'

'We were alive then.'

'I don't know about you but I'm still alive.'

'No, I mean we had no reason to doubt the future.'

'I still haven't got any reason to doubt the future. What about you?'

Rowney wondered if she really believed that. Did she really have any optimism left? She was in the middle of Hampshire with a man she hadn't seen in years, in a lonely cottage that was hosting a ghostly reunion of memories long buried. 'I don't know, I've stopped caring about it.'

'I guess that you haven't changed then, you never cared about the future back then either.'

'That's where you are wrong, I did care its just that I didn't let It show that's all.'

'What did you care about Chris? I mean really, never mind that the big top fell down and the whole thing crumbled in twenty short days, just tell me what it was that you cared about?'

'I thought that we would survive it, I thought that we would get through it that's all. It never even occurred to me that one tiny little problem would ever stop us. I didn't believe it was that fragile.'

'Well it was, and we both learned that. We both found out late that it wasn't right, that it wasn't meant to go further.'

'Don't do that, don't try and blame it on something beyond the sphere, when you say things like "it wasn't meant to go further" it only makes me angry because it pins the blame somewhere else. I know that isn't true because if you believe in things like that you give up control over your life, you're no longer in charge and that's a frightening thought.'

'Why can't you just leave it, Why has this gone on for so long? Why have you been out in the cold wandering in big circles Chris? Why have you tortured yourself? I didn't want this for either of us. I wanted both of us to be happy elsewhere. I wanted the both of us to find something new.'

'You did Cerys, you found something new, new and improved. You got yourself everything that I couldn't be. You found yourself a rich boy and a nice easy life.'

'That's not fair. I didn't marry Tom for his money.'

'Of course you didn't, that's why you followed him all the way down from Liverpool. That's why you kept in touch while you were still with me for a whole year before you walked out.'

'You're being childish, I was friends with Tom, and we had a lot in common.'

'Like what? What could you possibly have in common with that over fed brat? How can he even compare to you?'

'Tom is a good man, He's the right man and for the last half a decade he has been the only man. I can't help that and I can't help the past. Its gone no one can change it.'

'But I am and I have been. Do you think I spent all this time doing all the things I've done for the present or the future? You were my Future Cerys. I built my whole life around you. My plans started with you; before you I was just another face. I was having a good time and that was all there was.'

'I don't think I want to hear this. I don't want to know anymore, so please just stop.'

'Eight long years, eight long years I've chased and fought and kicked and screamed. There is nothing that I haven't done and little that I haven't seen. And none of it has ever been for my own benefit. Always I come back to you. I always come back to this. It's the only constant I have ever had.'

'You don't know what you're saying anymore Chris. You're in love with an idea, a fantasy, not a person. You are in love with yourself, your in love with a feeling that you had then. I'm not her anymore and you're not him. Those two were a pair of ragged children who didn't care about anything, their dreams were self contained. They only survived because they were isolated from the outside world. It was a cocoon we lived in. and the minute that you tried to turn into something real it fell apart.'

'No, it can still be had. Its not too late, it only fell apart because money strangled us both. But that isn't a problem anymore, we can be there forever, we can have that forever.'

'Why cant you understand that I don't want that anymore, I never wanted it to last forever, I wanted to grow up, I wanted to get out, I wanted to hurt and live and breathe outside of you. I wanted to feel alive. What we were doing wasn't living it was suffocation. It was slow suffocation.'

'Your wrong Cerys, we were more alive then anyone could possibly be. We breathed each other in and we had more then anyone could have asked for.'

'I want to go home Chris, I can't do this. I can't do this anymore. I have had this dream before and it always ends badly. Call your people I need to get back to the city.'

42

There were fourteen messages on the answer phone and eight of them were Tom's. The other six were from Aadam, work, Angelina, Aadam, Aadam and Moira's School.

After Cerys Deleted Tom's messages she called the other six. Angelina wasn't home and the school put her on hold, so she hung up hoping to call back later. Work was just a reminder on a deadline.

She rang Aadam last; the dwarf had a strange obsession with leaving messages and then rushing round to hear them himself.

'Hello Aadam?'

'Hi Crissy.'

'You left a couple of messages on my phone, Whats wrong?'

'I'm leaving, I've got a flight back to France in a few hours and I just wanted to let you know before I went.'

'When did you decide this? I thought you liked it here?'

'I do like it here its just that I have come into some money and I think I could do more with it over there then here.'

'Money? What do you mean? Did Tom?'

'Oh no, no, Tom had nothing to do with it. This Lawyer Rowley, I had an arrangement with, settled a debt for me that I had and it looks as though I won't have to stay in England anymore.'

'Did you just say Rowney?'

'Rowley, definitely Rowley; he promised to give me fifteen thousand pounds if I told him when and where you were going to be at certain times of the day. Kind of like a spy. Said he was some kind of tax official or something, was after you for evasion. I'm sorry to be the one to tell you this, but it looks as though I might have sold you out again Crissy.'

'I'm not evading any income tax? What? Wait a minute this man offered you fifteen thousand pounds to spy on me?'

'That's right, I thought it was pretty strange too, but you know how the rich are all a little mad. Take your husband, good lad but hoppy as frog shit. Writer? Who ever heard of something so stupid, if I were him I would have stuck with my dad and made a million or blown a million, whichever came first.'

'Wait Aadam you have to tell me what this man looked like?'

'Young guy, brown hair green eyes, Mick that's what I thought he was, a Mick, Irish that's what he made me think of.'

'Aadam wait I have to ask you some more things, where are you?'

'I'm, oh never mind. Look Crissy we had some good times didn't we? I mean Coney Island, remember that don't you. Playing on the big wheel, running through the sand. How many other transients do you know that can say that? Look, I know this might seem like betrayal but its not, I needed this badly. You don't know what it's been like for me the last couple of years. This money is going towards a better life for me. Who knows I might even write you a letter some time.'

The phone went dead; But Cerys was back on point.

43

Ashton road was a dump, but he was here at the behest of Azaz.

'Rowney, I want you to go to Cork. There's been a problem.'

In all his time here with Azaz Ireland was never an issue.

'One of our friends is in trouble and I want you to go and act as peacemaker.'

'I don't know anyone in Ireland, Why would you think I could resolve it? Why don't you go yourself?'

Azaz was in no mood. 'Here's your itinerary, there's a whole market out there that I have been delving and dabbling in.' Lies, lies, lies.

'I didn't know there was a game in Ireland; I didn't know you played over there?' It wasn't true; the Irish had no time for overseas investors.

'Well there is and right now there's a mistake that needs correcting I want you to go out there and un-fuck it for me.'

'Who do I get for company?'

'That's your choice entirely.'

'I have things to complete I don't have the'

'Whats the problem? You'll get a full report when you get there, but from what I've been told, a shipment has come in malnourished, I want you to track it and find out where the extra pound of flesh went.'

Azaz wasn't going to ask twice.

44

Cerys hadn't called back, the driver had dropped her outside of her house in Grady Street and that was the end of it.

Hubanach had gone back to the house to make amends and she had let him in. Chris had a man outside making reports, Cerys knew he was there and every so often stared at the big, black, conspicuous monstrosity hogging the pavement.

Hubanach was still unaware of what had been going on his absence.

'I just came to get a few things; I'll be out of your hair in five minutes.' Cerys didn't answer him as she stood in the doorway of the living room. 'I'll be upstairs.'

He went up to their bedroom and ran his hands through the drawers, quickly snatching at anything he might need, throwing them into a plastic Sainsbury's shopping bag. When the bag overflowed he wandered to the bathroom and grabbed his toothbrush. He looked around one last time; he didn't know how many excuses he could find after this one. He wanted so badly to go downstairs and say the right words. He wanted only to make this right, he wanted to change whatever it was, and he wished he hadn't left the house in the first place.

He went back down the stairs.

'Cerys? I'm all done.'

She looked away, she was still angry he could tell. And she wasn't going to engage in a prolonged argument just to satisfy his homesickness for a further ten minutes.

'I'll be going then.'

'He wanted her to look at him he wanted her to see the look on his face, he wanted her to acknowledge his hellish state, and he wanted her to see his remorse. But she wasn't going to and he knew it.

He went to the front door and closed it ever so slowly hoping that maybe she would walk over and invite him back in.

He was halfway down the street and looking back at every five paces before he realised that she was signalling him.

'We need to talk about this Tom; you have to tell me what the hell you have been doing?'

'I haven't done a thing Cerys.'

'It's a bit late for lies, I saw the tape, are you going to tell me that's a lie? I saw you do things that were just hideous.'

'Alright I was wrong, I don't know what happened and I don't know how I got in that tape but as far as I know I wasn't there, because I cant recall any of it. I don't know what you saw happen but I have no memory of it. I don't know anything about it.'

'Well you must because from what I saw you were very conscious.'

'I might have appeared conscious but that doesn't mean I was consenting.'

'Tom you were stupid enough to have someone make a tape and not only that; your friends or whoever they are, decided to post it through my letter box? What the hell does that mean? Does that mean that I'm going to be getting letters and photographs of you in leather straps for the rest of my life? Does this mean that I'm going to have to stand up in court and explain why I think you're an unsuitable parent? Because I don't want to do that. I'm upset Tom, I'm upset that even after everything we have, you still betrayed me.'

'Cerys, I would never betray.'

'But you did and you have, and I don't even know if this is the only time. How am I to know if you've been living some double life all along? Disappearing while I'm at work and getting up to all kinds of things; then coming home and pretending as though nothing is wrong?, doesn't that bother you in the slightest? Doesn't that make you wonder about yourself?'

'I've never done this before.'

How am I to know that? How am I to know?'

'By trusting me.'

'Trusting you? After this you want me to trust you?'

'I know it looks bad, but,'

'Looks bad? Is that what you think it does? She shrugged and walked to window. 'That video shows you doing things that I don't even want to say out loud.'

'It was one time and I think someone drugged me.'

'Who, Who drugged you?'

'I'll tell you everything if you let me explain without interruption.' And so he did.

He told her about the Cheltenham and the strange man that befriended him there. He told her about the collections agent Rowley.

'Did you say Rowney?'
'Rowley, Phillip Rowley.'
'What did he look like?'
'About thirty, brown hair hazel green eyes, medium height, well spoken.'
'What else happened?'
He went on to tell her about the H.H party and the strange gathering of people, he told her about the suit he had brought home and the assortment of drugged up models and call girls that wandered about in the private rooms.
'This man this Rowley what did he say he did for a living?'
'He said he was a collections agent in Burton.'
'Why did you go out with him if you didn't even know him? Why would you trust someone you have never met before? I don't understand why you'd do that?'
'I don't know?' Tom looked at the floor. 'You don't know what its like for me Cerys. All day trapped in this house with a Chilean maid for company who thinks children's television is the greatest invention on earth. You don't know what its like to butt heads with a typewriter all day only to have everyone laugh at your efforts because you have the money to support yourself. No one takes you seriously and no one even cares what you're thinking. I don't have any friends that aren't in my situation. Everyone I know is some

kind of invalid, I'm friends with retired couples and overgrown children like myself. Do you know how boring that is? I don't have any real friends; all I do is sit around waiting for something to happen.'

'And this was it?' she added

'I guess this Rowley guy was exactly what I was asking for, a friend that had some kind of real life, one that he wanted me to be a part of. Do you know how long it's been since I went out and just sat in a pub and had a beer with someone on their lunch break? It's been years. You know why it's been years because I sleep till lunch, I get up at one and can't drink till about four o clock. And you never said anything, you just let me drift out and pretend like I'm some kind of artist. Every one pushes me around because they think I'm just a rich waster and their right because I am, I just waste time, all of the time.'

'So your way of doing something productive was to cheat on me? Cheat on me with some drugged up hooker while a camera was rolling? That's life on the edge is it, and then getting it posted to your wife so she can throw you out? Is that some kind of dramatic search for meaning? To see if you could fuck up the only valid thing in your life?'

'No, Cerys I don't know why but I think I'm being black mailed.'

'You're being blackmailed? You really believe that? And who do you think they were going to send it to? Me, your father, or perhaps Jeremy Beadle. Don't be so stupid! If your looking for a reason, don't. You're stupidity got you caught. Going to drug parties in

chandelier ridden hotels with drugged up hookers. If that's not grounds for divorce I don't know what is. All I know is that there is something behind this and I'm going to find out.'
 Whats behind this all Cerys?'
 'Nevermind, now that you have explained yourself you can go. I'm going to be sending a letter to Mr Willimer and we will be discussing this further in his company Tom, so just be aware of that.'

45

The tube was overflowing, there were barely a handrail to hold and the ground had more leather then ground on it. Rowney had his back to the exit and he was sure that someone's hand was in his pocket. On his face the breath of a giant man was hot and dull, thank goodness the man was not a smoker or a garlic enthusiast; He was aware of his position and had nobly stuck a fresh stick of chewing gum there. But that didn't stop the stench coming from his armpits, Rowney and the woman to his left were very aware of that.

Behind him was an annoyed young man with a scowl that reflected on both opposing windows. Even with the over abundance of bodies the man's scowl was clearly visible.

The train was heading west through the ribs of the city and Rowney felt as though he was passing through some beasts kidney's, the hot perspiration and the smell of piss water in the air convinced him of that much. He wanted badly to check his telephone to see if she had called, even though he was underground and his telephone didn't work; he still waited for something to happen.

The tube train stopped and a tiny little man got off only for ten more to take his place. Rowney squeezed up against an old woman who didn't want anyone near her. In the corner a well dressed black lady rested against a cushioned seat placed at the far edge of the carriage. The doorway meant that between journeys she had the luxury of not having someone's arm pit in her face and for this affront, the standing passengers glared with envy.

'It wasn't long before the tube train had taken onboard too many. Rowney knew that for the remainder four stops till the thing left the heart of zone one it would remain like this. He wasn't going to see daylight for at least thirty minutes and if he was going to lose his freedom for thirty minutes he might as well push up against the back wall of the tube and pretend he was somewhere else.

Sayby was over head on the road, he was sitting behind the wheel of an old hatchback, and it was spewing out black smoke and looked like a dinosaur in a pigeon coop. He was wearing the most expensive tie had ever bought. He bought it simply because he could and that's what he had said when the retailer had advised a paisley to go with his shirt. He had a bad habit of doing that. Going into a place and buying something simply because he could, simply as an expression of how great it was to be on the top wrung. It didn't matter how you got there all that mattered was being there and Sayby was definitely there.

The car however was a cover vehicle, it belonged to a man on Heston boulevard and was full of watered down London brand. Sayby had taken it from a shipment that had just been unloaded in Woking and was bound for Yorkshire, Sayby had decided to take a bail for himself. Rowney was supposed to be supervising but for some reason unknown to everyone except Rowney, he hadn't been there. So

Sayby covered for him. He took a blacked out Mercedes and parked a quarter mile away on a high spot telling the buyers that Rowney would watch from there. Azaz was unaware of the scam, and as far as he was concerned the sale went on without any problems.

Sayby had tried to call Rowney but it had been a bad day for responses, the operations were all going over without problems, even if the head was off the shoulders.

Garret had to be in Gatesmoor in an hour and if Rowney was going to be elusive for the next few days then all the better for Sayby.

46

She wondered. 'Did you think I wouldn't find out, was that it?'

'Find what out.'

'You know perfectly well what I'm talking about.' Between the hiss and crackle of mobile phone interference it was a sure thing, the game was up.

'Phillip Rowley? Do you know anyone by that name?'

'Never heard of him.'

'Well you should, because a man with that name drugged my husband and tried to wreck my marriage, He also went to great lengths to find a dwarf in France to come and spy on me!' She was screaming down the phone 'I don't know what in the hell you were playing at, but if you ever come near me or my family again, I'm going to get in touch with the police.'

'Really Cerys, is that what you're going to do? Well you see, I've grown fond of video camera's in the past few years. I've always loved the idea of looping a life over and over. The idea of seeing your own actions being replayed infinitely for the benefit of some viewer somewhere fascinates me. That's why I made a tape.'

'You made a tape of what.'

'Marchman house, I wired a camera to the rooms so that way I wouldn't have to ever forget you again. All I have to do now is pop it into the video player every time I get lonely for you. In fact I even made a copy especially for friends like yourself and Tom. So think about that before you try and threaten me.'

'You're lying, you're trying to make me afraid of you, well I'm not Chris, you're a sad lonely man who never let go of his hang ups, your pathetic, and if you ever thought that I would leave my husband for you then you don't know me at all.'

'I know you Cerys, I've known you for longer then you or I could imagine. This was supposed to happen, to see if it was real; if you hadn't of disappeared I would have never known. If you hadn't lost touch with me I would have never valued you. It was only without you that I saw how lost I was. And now I know what to do about it.'

'Nothing Chris, that's what you're going to do, nothing. You're going to stay away. You're going to stay away from me and my family, your going to leave me alone. And I don't believe your shit about a tape; even you wouldn't do a thing like that.'

47

The capital was a long corridor of ugly rooms, and on the last day of January Christopher Rowney held residence in the ugliest room. The wallpaper hadn't been changed since 1987 and the smell of the last man to have died here, lingered like the ghost of pot pourri.

He was preparing to board an Aer Lingus flight, away from the island to the Ireland. All he needed was a phone call from Azaz and an okay on the location. Cork city airport was hardly going to be the depot; it was more likely to be some arse ended farm house that was doubling as a factory.

The grey flat television that was operated on coins long ago made obsolete, sat still in the corner and Rowney folded a shirt into a small brown suitcase. He hung his red leather coat on the back of a beaten up chair and kept the curtains closed to the last flickers of daylight.

He was promised a phone call and that was all he really desired. The winter had been unkind when the autumn had held such promise. He had spent this eighth year in the hope of some success or failure but here he was unable to recognize either one.

The idea that Cerys had finally decided otherwise was too much to take. The notion that he had over played his hand was a conceit he refused to accept.
"There's always a chance, there's always."

Wagner's ride of the Valkyrie's blared in a heartless electronic mobile telephone clone.

'Hello?'

'Rowney, come to the shop, I need to see you there's been a change of plan.'
'Whats wrong Azaz? Whats happened.'
'Nothing just get here, I've got a few things to talk about.'
'Fine I'll be there in an hour.'

*

It was sinful to close a store midweek that said "open seven days" on the overhead sign. The shutters of the Kadiz general store were rolled down and the cars that normally cluttered the alleyway beside it had magically disappeared. For some reason, as dusk came down, Rowney stood alone in polished shoes on Ashton Road. For once he was apprehensive.

He looked around for any signs of life but found none. Even the neighbouring stores had rolled down shutters and the houses across the street looked deserted. The death of the usually busy traffic was also in league with Azaz. The whole world stood silent.

Rowney walked to the back of the Stores side alley and looked up to the flat windows that hovered over the rear yard. A dim light flickered where Azaz usually sat and the fire escape that led upward loomed in front of him, daring him to climb up.

He put his feet on the step and took the rise to the door.

Azaz was waiting.

The fat brown man swung open the door and stuck out his hands; he grabbed Rowney by the collar and dragged him in before he could make a sound. He dumped him on the stink ridden sofa and looked down at him from his giant's height, bathed in the dim orange glow.

'You decided to come.'

'What the fucks wrong with you.' Rowney had been around Azaz so long that he had almost forgotten the brute force that sat under sagging skin. He was a fat old man, but that didn't diminish the trace of the monster he once was.

'Nothing, just waking you up that's all. Want to watch a video? I've got just the "one" for you.'

Azaz pulled a remote control from his pocket and pointed it backwards at the video, playing a grainy security film showing a man unloading a van.

'Whats this?'

'This my friend is you, its you at the Dock-land warehouse last December 12th. It shows you unloading a van full of my stock and reloading it with two cases missing. Now would you like to explain to me why you accidentally lost two cases of my stock?'

'I don't know what you're talking about. I never stole from you?'

'So that handsome man on screen isn't you?'

'It is me but I'm not stealing anything, those boxes you see me taking away are my own private buys. The stock count said ten but if you look through the amount of boxes I unload there are twelve. The two I take for myself are extras that I ordered for my own interests.'

'And you think that somehow makes it all ok? You think it's smoothed over.' The fat old man put his hands on his hips and smiled viciously. 'You think that's ok do you?' the boot drove in to Rowney's shin bone, then it raised higher up into his stomach. 'You think that putting an extra charge on my shipment is somehow alright, you think that me paying excesses that I'm not even aware of is acceptable, you little bastard.'

The curled breathless heap on the floor managed to beggar an explanation. 'I never stole from you! I never did, not even once. Not even when it was easy did I steal from you. All the things I bought under your name I paid for and put back the original costs from my own pockets, in fact I even put half of my profits back into your work. I never robbed you, and I never even dreamed of betrayal.'

The giant towered over the crumpled man. 'How do I know you're not lying? How the fuck do I know you're not Bull shitting me!' You thieving Scouse bastard! How the fuck do I know?'

Rowney looked up from the floor, with whimpering fear flushing his face. 'Because I wouldn't you stupid old fuck! Of all the people in this hellish city, you're the only one who looked out for me. After all the shit I went through with those Antique gangsters you were the only one that let me work without bleeding me dry. You helped me when I was a leper and do you think that I would betray you? Did you ever think I would do that to you of all people? Think about it Azaz. I haven't had it this good since I was in Liverpool. And that's almost a lifetime away.'

'You're a fucking liar! You always were. What about that Paki crack-head, that Reza.'

'Reza's a nobody; I keep him on my personal payroll like a side project to see how far I can push someone through the maze. I wanted to push out the boat and see if I could survive on the ground with just one team of supply and distribution.'

'Why would you want to waste your time? I don't understand why you would want to waste time with distribution? We make more money on wholesale, it's the smart mans move to stay with bigger options. Why would you want to get back into that ground floor mess?'

'Because I'm curious, Curious about how far I can go before someone notices. I want to know what happens next. I've been doing this for so long that it feels like a waste of life, I have no one to answer to except you and I live a life that goes unquestioned, and what for? I've got nothing. There's nobody, I've got fuck all. Just money! All the money any one could want and nothing to do with any of it.'

'What about this Woman this bloody woman you've been getting Sayby to follow round, don't think I didn't know about that, you took her to some place in Hampshire last week. I spent two days trying to get hold of you and you were off shagging some bloke's wife! What the bloody hell is wrong with you?'

'Leave that out of it. That's got nothing to do with you.'

'When you pull my men off real jobs and have them spy on some posh tart then it becomes my business. You can't expect my team to just dance whenever you get fiddlers itch! You can't just fuck my day up because you feel like it.'

Rowney climbed back onto the sofa. With a hand on his knee he tried to rub the black stain that was left by the giant boot. 'I wasn't messing with your day I wasn't trying to spoil your operation. The women in Grady Street was a friend of mine once, I knew her in Liverpool.'

'Wait a minute? So this bird, oh fuck no! Don't give me that shit! I was warned of this. When I first met you I got told about how you got into this in the first place! Your old boss warned me about the bird who fucked your whole life, Karen or Kerry or something one of those dark Gippo looking birds. God, you found her didn't you, you stupid bastard, and what did you do? Oh no, don't fucking tell me.'

'What I do in my time.'

'Your wrong, none of it's your time, I own you, and I'm going to own you till I think that it's the right time to let you out of the canary cage. You don't seem to understand the magnitude of the favour I offered you. When those old villains cast you out, they put a price on your head. They hired you out to me for a grand sum of two hundred and fifty thousand pounds. Didn't you ever wonder why no one would touch you with a barge pole? Too much risk. So I put the money up and brought you on board. Now I covered the debt with fifteen years worth of serious labour, that's not something charmed or imagined, the things I did for that money I don't even want to remember. But I put it all on you and thank fuck you paid off. Now four years later I'm one of the richest untaxed bastards in the cricket playing universe.'

'Then why don't you let me out, that's all I want. I want to disappear. I want to go away.'

'You are going away Rowney. You see I've spent the last few weeks collecting information as to if and why you've been robbing me. I came to the conclusion that you were and my way of dealing with it was to go to all of your little investments and burn them down with the Tenant's still inside. So as of this evening you stand to lose three quarters of a million pound in property and five hundred thousand pounds in movable assets.'

Chris wiped the face that he thought bloody, when all that ran from his nose was a mixture of snot and tears. 'What makes you think I'm going to give you my movable assets? That's my life and I'm not going to give you anything not a single fucking penny you fat bastard.'

'Well Rowney the problem is that Mr Mill, you know Mr Mill from Cardiff? Well he got a bad shipment. So bad in fact that he didn't really want to keep it. Now he had to dump one hundred thousand pounds of defective goods in the sea front because it's as good as detergent. After all of his transporting and siphoning costs, he rounded up the figure to three hundred thousand pounds in refundable cash. Now I don't know how he came to that ludicrous figure so I protested and gave him your name. There was no way I was going to pay it so I made it fair on you, I knew that you had money lying around in various places and since it was your fault that someone watered the shipment down to make it appear overweight. I think it's only fair that you should bear the burden of refunding Mr Mill.'

'So you set a crazy Welsh man on me thinking you could get my money and cover your own arse at the same time?'

'That's about right yes.'

'Sorry no, I don't believe you.'

'Believe what you want, but as of this moment four of his men are headed here for you. There going to take you out to a quiet location and make you pay the debt in full, with whatever methods they see fit. It was either you or me Chris and I thought "he's a single man, hasn't got any family or real interests beyond the financial, so let it be him" fairs fair after all.'

'Besides the benefit of breathing, what else do I get? You can't expect me to be your lap dog after you rip me off Azaz? I mean even you have got more brains then that.'

'Complete freedom and banishment. You leave the country with whatever you have in your pockets right now. So that's an Aer Lingus ticket and a few shirts. Go and see Ireland, you're always going on about it. I'm giving you your chance.'

'If I agree, whats to stop you from just shooting me yourself?'

'What would I get from that? I've known you a lot of years Chris, contrary to what you might believe I have a lot of respect for you and in some ways I'm quite envious. You have that rare ability to snap out of any situation no matter how bad it is. The amount of times I've seen and heard about you turning some failed venture into a thriving bloody goldmine is astounding. Take your latest for example, That junkie who's probably roasting right now in the house I had burnt down, was turning over three thousand pound a week on one telephone and no car. Do you know how hard it is to even contemplate a figure like that on foot with out any help from anyone else? I used to do it years ago and that kind of money doesn't exist for anyone but the established few. But he managed it in a few weeks just with you behind him. And that's how I know that you'll bounce back.'

'What am I supposed to do out in the middle of Ireland beg for change? Or better yet do a jig for a few Euro's? Get friendly with the Irish and hope they need a cast off to run their operations for them? Come on Azaz, if you want me out then let me have the money I've made and I'll be out of your hair, just give me an hour and you will never hear from me again.'

'You see Chris, I'm giving you five minutes to make up your mind. Either way this will probably be the last time that we ever see each other. So think fast.' The old fat man had won, just like he always said he did.

Strange pointers.

48

It was a hard month; March had been all polite in the private study of Mr Willimer, the family solicitor. He had managed with his ethereal presence to deter any flights of emotion that Cerys might have felt needed airing. Any mention of Call girls and Amphetamines were passed over and it was called simple infidelity.

'He was unfaithful and that was part of our agreement. If either of us failed to oblige the few simple requirements then this whole arrangement was to be dissolved.'

She didn't look at him once, even when she got up to leave, she deliberately avoided Tom at all costs.

But that didn't matter, because March was over and today was the Day of the fool.

The first of April, that horrible beautiful month that we can all stomach but can't stand.

April.

For Tom a Dublin April.

Drumcondra Road was the throat of the capital. It led to the bowels of the city and to the left of it sat the dock Harbour, almost like a Liverpool in reverse.

Tom was not as wealthy as he thought he was, His father had been smart enough to bring out the big guns, he had strangled the trust fund down to the bare essentials, it had drawn itself out of the lofty clouds and was down to a few hundred pounds a month, a lot for a teenager living on coffee and cigarettes, which was precisely what Tom was, a childish man branded by his own indolence.

He hadn't seen Cerys since March and he was in some ways relieved. She had ignored him since their last conversation in January and at the private counsel hearing in Willimer's office she ignored his attempts at direct conversation. She had been kind enough to remain as vague as possible about the nature of his indiscretions but her indifference stung more then any sordid detail revealed.

His stay in Dublin was dressed in the intentions of escapism but he had been here for less then a day and already regretted. He had come with the express notion of a break from his own tunnelled existence, but in the grown city he felt no difference. On the broad walks that for some brought out old wars and beautiful songs, he only received cold remembrance of his wife's drab London.

He sat down in a public house by the Drumcondra train station and rued the winter that had robbed him. He thought over the last six that went before and how he had sometimes dreamt of some small change that would mark out a year among so many that were alike in dullness. He had sat at his word processor with the dream of some spark; the hope of some new lightning bolt to charge him full of fire, but it never came.

Here on the lonely foreign road in a pub that smelled of yeast and not Tobacco, he saw that he had always been wrong to mock the things he had.

Somewhere far away, the daughter that was never really his played alone, forgetting something about daddy every day. Somewhere the wife that that was never really his, was wondering who she would spend her life with next; and out there somewhere a lizard in an expensive suit slithered around rocks looking for something new to destroy.

He had not given up on Rowley. In February he had hired an investigator to find the man but it came back blank, so he took to the shell of the rooms that he had visited and badgered the hotel reception till they allowed him to see the registration and payment details of the Harris Hawk party.

It took him down a blind alley. It was registered in the name of a Garret j Sayby. He gave the name Sayby to a private investigator and again it turned up nothing. Sayby, a south London Landlord and fabric wholesaler, had never heard the name Rowley.

So on the finger nail of Europe, behind a decrepit glass of beer; Thomas Hubanach thought about staying for a while. After, all Ireland was the one place that had never drawn him. It had always seemed too close, too similar to home for it ever to appeal. He was here now because he had found a flight that cost one pound and a hotel room that cost fifteen. It was a sad thing to admit but budgeting had finally infected him, Divorce was making sure of that.

He nodded at the barman and decided to walk into the city.

Behind the trees and in the distance from Drumcondra, Tom had seen a giant needle touching the sky. He didn't know where its base sat since he hadn't bothered, in his ignorance, to buy a map or a tourists guide at the airport. He decided to find the needles feet.

April was not kind in Ireland, the isle and the city caught the gust and the rush of air from the sea. It blew away the dead of winter and awakened nerves to the coming heat of the next season.

All along the wide berth of road the loose plastic bags danced away from rubbish bins and up on old churches, weather vanes played merry go round alone on the heights.

Tom kept walking. He had crossed two bridges in search of the needle and he could see the point sharpening before his eyes. From the distance he had thought it to be the spire of some great church raised high above the city to proclaim Rome mightiest of all, but from the second bridge he knew it to be a needle.

The people that were spread thin on Drumcondra were coming away from the hidden rooms of the city. The pulse of living thoughts swelled toward the centre where the needle sat sabre like in the chest of great Dublin. The Englishman walked on past the over wrought buildings and the grate rails of a long dead empire. He walked through the old marsh of a battle field in the middle of a street and saw the ghosts that peered out at the lost foreigner in their midst.

He stared at the ancient signs that read of the Gaelic tongue and left him alien and outside. He stumbled for the roads and wondered if he was chasing his own tail, he then looked up at the needle and knew that he was near.

All around him the voices grew stronger till he couldn't hear the drone of his own skull any longer, the irrepressible names of his wife and child were fading as the foreign tongue that he and his kind had tried so long to destroy with good grammar and endless repetition, overtook him. The thick Gael voices drummed out of the faces marching past. Here in this strange familiar place, in this place of unending revolt; this last corner of the civilised world, this last place of unfamiliar memories.

Then, it was clear. The needle became itself on a wide coronation street, alongside mighty statues of men that he didn't know. Names stood hardened for him to say or sing out loud; Men's names that had left behind a memory wiser then thought or reliance.

He stood at the base of the needle and looked up to where the tip disappeared; he wished that he had brought a camera; something, anything to have recorded it. To have been able to document the lack and loss of something as it is gradually replaced by something else; something new.

Here on the shore of the island of Ireland he had forgotten for one moment; that he was about to dissolve, that everything around him was melting away. If he could have had anything, if he could have chosen one moment to stretch out over the entirety of his existence; he would have claimed a cold April morning on O'Connell Street.

Tom looked around as the people stared at the obvious tourist. He looked around for others like himself, others that were marvelling, but there were none.

Except one,
Further down the road he caught sight of a lizard walking toward him. A lizard wearing a smile like a tailored suit..